URBAN OUTLAWS

'The BEST BOOK EVER. I loved the cool gadgets and how they always get caught but manage to escape. Slink is my favourite character'
Ollie, aged 10

'I have finally found a near-equal to the Harry Potter series. It's right here – *Urban Outlaws*'
Frankie, aged 9

'Jam-packed with the latest tech and gadgets and inspires kids like me to become skilled and cool like the characters. This book was a bit like *CHERUB*…BRILLIANT'
Lewis, aged 12

'I really enjoyed *Urban Outlaws* because it is about children who lead an exciting underground life, free from rules and parents. My favourite character is Charlie because she is *REALLY COOL* and can do everything the boys can do, just a lot better!'
Scarlett, aged 9

'I loved the fast-paced thrill of the action and the idea of living in a secret bunker. I enjoyed it so much I wish it was longer!'
Sam, aged 12

'It is a 10 out of 10 book. I hope there is another one and, if there is, I will be first in line to buy it!'
Jack, aged 9

'An adventure-packed book full of amazing twists and characters . . . The main characters are a group of nobodies put together by fate and so you feel as if you are part of the book more'
Luke, aged 13

'I enjoyed this book because there was lots of machinery and action. It was fast-paced, never standing still at all, which made it very exciting . . . This book definitely goes into my top ten'
Milo, aged 10

'A gripping read with many twists in the story. It is a mix of *Fantastic Four* and *CHERUB*. I recommended the book to some of my friends and, after they read it, they said that they loved it as well'
Tom, aged 13

We want to hear what you think!
Tweet your reviews to @kidsbloomsbury using
#urbanoutlaws
or email us at **childrensmarketing@bloomsbury.com**

URBAN OUTLAWS LOCKDOWN

PETER JAY BLACK

BLOOMSBURY

LONDON OXFORD NEW DELHI NEW YORK SYDNEY

Bloomsbury Publishing, London, Oxford, New York, New Delhi and Sydney

First published in Great Britain in September 2015 by Bloomsbury Publishing Plc
50 Bedford Square London WC1B 3DP

www.bloomsbury.com

A CIP catalogue record for this book is available from the British Library

ISBN 978 1 4088 5147 0

Typeset by Integra Software Services Pvt. Ltd.
Printed and bound in Great Britain by CPI Group (UK) Ltd, Croydon CR0 4YY

1 3 5 7 9 10 8 6 4 2

For Kirsty

CHAPTER ONE

JACK FENTON WATCHED OVER CHARLIE'S shoulder as she used her set of customised tools to pick the lock on the metal door. The train rocked from side to side and he hoped she'd factored the motion into her timings.

After a few more anxious seconds, Jack peered through the other door behind them to the passenger carriage beyond.

All was quiet in there – people were reading newspapers, listening to iPods, oblivious to what was going on.

Hopefully it would stay that way.

His eyes drifted to the far end of the carriage, where Wren was sitting in an aisle seat. Her long, blonde hair was tied up with a pink bow and she looked like an innocent ten-year-old.

A deception.

Jack caught her eye and whispered into his head-set, 'You doing OK?'

Wren smiled and gave a slight nod.

Jack stayed as still as possible, letting Charlie get on with her work.

He turned to the compartment's side window, watched the trees and houses speed past and quickly ran through the rest of the mission – checking for any last-minute problems.

The security door Charlie was working on had a special lock. Beyond that door was an armoured train carriage. And in that carriage was a silver briefcase.

Jack had no idea what was inside the briefcase, and right at that moment he didn't care. All he knew was a man called 'the Shepherd' wanted it. In exchange for the briefcase, this Shepherd guy would help the Outlaws get from London to New York.

Jack balled his fists as he thought of Hector.

Hector was their new enemy. He'd managed to copy the world's most advanced virus and he was now taking the virus apart to understand how it worked. He intended to use it to become the great-est hacker ever known.

Hector would then be free to do whatever he wanted. Just like his father – he'd steal secrets and sell them to the highest bidder. He'd cause chaos and misery wherever he went. And – Jack's stomach twisted – with that sort of power, given time, Hector could even track down the location of the Urban Outlaws' bunker.

Using a program Jack had written, the Outlaws had tracked Hector to America. That was why they needed to get to New York, and *fast*.

Jack's gaze moved back to the security door.

First things first, he told himself. They needed that briefcase.

'Sixteen minutes before you reach the train station,' a voice said in their ears. Obi was back at the bunker, watching the CCTV footage and keeping an eye out for any police or bad guys.

Charlie was still working on the lock. Beads of sweat trickled off her forehead and down her cheeks. She didn't seem to notice – the concentration on her face was intense.

Jack didn't want to interrupt her, but sixteen minutes meant they were running out of time. She should've been done with the lock by now. He leant in. 'How you doin'?'

'Not good,' Charlie hissed back. 'It's tougher than I thought.'

She'd practised on a similar lock back at the bunker until she could do it blindfolded, but this one seemed to be a newer version.

Upgrades, Jack thought. *That's all we need.*

He braced himself. 'So, how long?'

Charlie puffed a strand of hair from her eyes. 'I'm going as quick as I can.' Her voice sounded strained, but, as always, she seemed in control.

Jack straightened up and cupped a hand over his microphone. 'Slink?' A blast of dubstep almost tore Jack's eardrums from his skull. He winced. 'Slink. *Seriously?*'

After a few seconds the music died down.

'What?'

'Do you have to do that, like, *every* time?'

'Yeah, mostly,' Slink said. 'And?'

Obi chuckled.

'Come on, guys, I'm trying to work here.' Charlie shook her head and returned her attention to the lock.

Jack stepped away from her and whispered into his mic, 'Slink, just tell us where you are.'

'All right, chill your beans. That guy's finally gone, and I'm getting into position. I'll have it all set up for you in the next couple of minutes.' He'd been delayed too.

Wren cleared her throat.

Now what?

Jack spun to the passenger carriage door.

Through the window he could see a conductor walking down the aisle towards them, asking for tickets as he went.

'Charlie?' Jack didn't take his eyes off the man. 'I don't mean to rush you, but we kinda need an ETA here.'

'At least a few minutes more.'

Minutes?

Jack gauged they had less than sixty seconds before the conductor reached them. 'We don't have that much time.'

Charlie glanced up at him. 'If I stop now, I'll have to start all over again. And that would mean another fifteen minutes at least.'

'Not a chance, you guys,' Obi said through the headset. 'The station is now fourteen minutes away.'

As soon as the train pulled into the station, the armoured carriage would be unloaded and they'd have no way to get that silver briefcase.

Brilliant.

Jack ground his teeth.

The conductor only had six more tickets to check before he came through the compartment door and found them.

'*Charlie?*' Jack said out of the corner of his mouth.

'Wait.'

Four tickets.

Jack glanced at Wren – she was wringing her hands and staring intently at him.

Two tickets.

'Time's up,' Jack whispered into his microphone. 'Wren, execute *Operation Decoy*.'

As the conductor reached for the button on the door, Wren leapt to her feet and *screamed*.

The conductor wheeled round, his mouth hanging open in shock.

Several passengers turned in their seats to gawk at her too.

Wren's eyes were wide and panicked.

The conductor came to his senses and started walking towards her, his hands outstretched, while saying something Jack couldn't make out.

That should buy them the few extra minutes they needed.

'Well done, Wren.' Jack turned to Charlie as, to his utter surprise, she straightened up and stepped back from the security door. 'You've done it?' he said.

'Yes, but –' Charlie let out a puff of frustration and glanced away.

Jack had that sudden sinking feeling.

He looked between Charlie and the security door. 'But...what?'

'I'm sorry, Jack. I had no way of knowing.'

'Knowing what?' He frowned. 'What are you talking about?'

Charlie looked at him. 'I've unlocked the door, but it won't open. There must be a bolt on the inside or something.'

Jack's blood ran cold as realisation hit him. 'Wait – does that mean someone's in there?'

Charlie shook her head. 'I don't think so. If there was, they'd have heard me picking the lock and come to investigate already.'

That was a good point. 'Then how do they get in –' Jack winced. 'Oh, no.'

Now he understood – on the side of the armoured carriage was another door that the workers used to load and unload the contents on to the station platform. With this inner door to the compartment bolted, the side door was the only way in or out of there.

'Twelve minutes, guys,' Obi said over their headsets.

'I'm really sorry,' Charlie said.

'It's not your fault.'

Charlie sighed. 'What do you want to do?' she said in a small voice. 'Should we get off the train at the station?'

'There has to be another way.' Jack's mind raced for a solution.

He looked into the passenger compartment.

Wren was now on the floor, rolling around as if she was possessed, while the conductor was standing over her looking unnerved.

'Wait a minute.' Jack glanced at Charlie and pointed to the compartment's external side door. 'You can open this without the driver or conductor knowing, right?'

They'd planned to use the external door when they made their escape. Normally it was impossible to open those doors until the train had stopped, but Charlie had a way around it.

She frowned. 'Yeah.'

'And you have the signal jammer?'

'Yep. Why?'

Jack slipped off his hard-shell backpack and pulled out two oversized suction cups with handles. They each had a small motor, and pipes ran to the cups.

They'd planned to use the grippers at the end of the mission, just before they reached the station, but Jack couldn't think of any other way to do this in the time they had left. He held them up. 'Will they hold?'

Charlie's eyes widened as she understood what he was getting at. 'I designed them for use at thirty or forty miles an hour.' She glanced out of the window as the train continued to speed along the track. 'We must be going well over a hundred.'

'Eleven minutes,' Obi said.

Jack slipped his hands through the loops on the handles. 'No choice.'

Charlie pulled the signal jammer – a black rectangle, ten centimetres long by four wide – from her hip bag. It had a stubby antenna at one end and a small display.

She switched it on, stuck it to the wall, then spoke into her headset. 'Obi?'

'Here.'

Good. She could still communicate with them. Charlie had set the device to block all mobile phone and radio signals. All but the one they were using.

She looked at Jack. 'Are you sure about this?'

Jack nodded. 'Do it.'

Charlie went across to the side door.

Next to it was a panel. She opened it and removed an internal cover, revealing a circuit board with a modification she'd made earlier.

She pressed a button and a light came on inside. 'OK. Ready.'

Jack hesitated and glanced back towards the passenger compartment. 'Can you keep this door closed?'

It hadn't been an issue before – if the conductor had spotted them leaving the train, it would've been too late for him to do anything about it. Especially with the phone signals blocked.

'I can cut the power to all the doors,' Charlie said. 'But the conductor has a key to open them manually.'

'What about the emergency brakes?'

'It's risky, but I can disconnect the power to them too. The driver shouldn't have any idea what's going

10

on, and the passengers will be trapped in the compartment with no way to call the police.'

Jack peered into the carriage again. 'Right.'

Wren was still on the floor. Her eyes had rolled back and she was convulsing.

Jack couldn't help but smile – she was a good actress.

A few passengers were holding phones up, trying desperately to get a signal.

'Wren, listen,' Jack said. 'The conductor has a key in his pocket and we need it.'

Wren's eyes suddenly flew open and she leapt to her feet.

The conductor scrambled back in surprise as Wren ran forward. He grabbed her and for a few moments they wrestled, but Wren managed to duck under his arms and slip past.

Jack hit the button on the door. It slid open and Wren ran through. As it closed again, Charlie cut the power.

The guard pressed the button too, but it didn't open again. He looked confused and rummaged in his pockets.

Wren held up the key and grinned at Jack.

'Good work.'

'Ten minutes,' Obi said.

Jack turned away. They were almost out of time. 'Open it,' he said to Charlie.

She handed him a set of lock picks. 'You're really sure about this?'

'No,' Jack said, slipping them into his pocket, 'but if we don't complete this mission...' He groaned, thinking of the consequences if they didn't stop Hector. 'I'm all out of ideas,' he said in a resigned tone. 'This is our only chance.'

Charlie, seemingly aware that she didn't have a better plan either, said, 'Good luck,' and pressed a switch on the circuit board.

The side door opened and wind whipped through the compartment, almost knocking them off their feet.

The conductor banged on the glass. 'What the 'ell are you doing?' his muffled voice shouted.

Jack ignored him and gripped the yellow pole by the door to steady himself.

He took three quick breaths, pulled his bandana and hood up, then leant out.

The wind instantly tried to pluck him from the compartment, but Jack managed to press the first gripper to the smooth painted surface of the outside of the train.

He hit a button under his thumb. The gripper's motor engaged and Jack felt the suction cup depress under his hand.

He gave the gripper a tug, making sure it was secure and, after a couple more deep breaths, hauled himself out the door and into the open.

For a moment Jack hung there, and it took all his strength not to be torn from the train.

Trying not to think too much, he shifted his weight, reached up as high as he could with the second gripper, and, arms burning, dragged himself up the outside of the carriage.

Now his head was just below the curve of the roof. He could make out Obi's faint voice in his ear, but because of the wind, and the heavy pounding in his chest, it was hard to hear what he was saying.

It sounded like, 'Eight minutes.'

Jack considered giving up and lowering himself back down through the door, but then he reminded himself of what rested on the outcome of this mission.

No silver briefcase, no tickets to America, no stopping Hector.

A tree shot past him and its branches brushed his jacket.

'All right, all right, I'm going,' he muttered to himself as he released the lower gripper and reached up beyond the top curve of the train carriage.

He found the flat part of the roof, pressed the gripper's button and felt it tighten. Only then did he release the second gripper and haul himself up and on to the roof of the train carriage, keeping his head low and his face pressed to the cold metal.

Wind ripped at Jack's clothes. It felt as though a thousand hands were slapping him, trying to prise him off.

With every bit of determination he had, Jack lifted his head and squinted into the wind. He would have to crawl halfway along the carriage, and it seemed like a million miles.

With his eyes watering, Jack reached forward and secured the other gripper, then bent his knees and forced himself along the roof.

Suddenly the train punched into a tunnel and his ears popped.

Disorientated and in the darkness, with wind clawing at every inch of his body, Jack remembered the safety and the warmth of the bunker and wished he was back there.

He continued forward in the dark – one gripper in front of the other – until the tunnel finally released the train into the light and he looked up. Tears streamed down his face and he could just make out the top of the armoured side door a metre ahead.

Jack quickly pulled himself towards it and peered over the edge.

The door below was divided into two halves, secured with a hefty-looking padlock.

Jack reached down, attached one gripper to the side of the door and let go of the other.

Hanging on with only one hand, he felt in his pocket for the lock picks and slid two out of their wallet.

It was then that it hit him – he would need both hands to pick a lock - one to use the rake, the other to apply pressure on the wrench.

He swore.

'Five minutes,' Obi's voice said faintly, as if he were just back in that tunnel.

Jack swore again and glanced up at the gripper he'd left on the edge of the roof. He had an idea.

A bad idea, but he was desperate.

Jack rotated his body, reached up with one foot and slipped it through the loop on the gripper above him.

He yanked a few times, making sure it was secure, then let go with both hands and hung upside down.

This had to be the stupidest thing he'd ever done.

Jack started to work on the lock.

It was slow going – normally Charlie would be doing this, or even Slink. Jack hadn't picked a lock since his time at the children's home.

Mind you, he'd like to see either of them trying to do it in these conditions – like a bat in a wind tunnel.

The train rocked as it passed over a set of points.

Pain shot through Jack's leg and he winced, but he managed to keep going – raking the lock and putting pressure on the wrench.

Finally, as if by some miracle, the padlock sprang open.

He removed it and slid one of the doors open, holding on to the edge of it.

Freeing his foot, Jack dropped as far as he could, then swung into the train and collapsed on to the floor.

The relief was instantaneous.

He lay there for a few seconds, breathing hard, happy to be alive.

His face tingled as the feeling returned, and he blinked away the tears.

'Jack,' Obi's anxious voice said. 'You've got four minutes left until you reach the station.'

Four minutes? Jack thought. *Is that all?*

He jumped to his feet and unbolted the door at the end of the security carriage.

A relieved-looking Charlie and Wren were waiting for him in the compartment beyond.

'Where's the case?' Charlie said.

'The what?'

She pushed past him and her eyes scanned the shelves. 'There.' Charlie reached up and grabbed a silver briefcase.

Jack had been so shocked to have made it into the compartment that he'd forgotten about it.

'Can we open it?' Wren said.

'Not enough time,' Jack said. 'We'll be at the station in a few minutes.'

Jack and Charlie hurried to the carriage's side door and helped Wren up to the gripper he had left on the roof.

The wind was dying down and it was easier for her to make progress. After an uneasy few moments, Wren's feet disappeared.

'Jack.' Charlie pointed.

A couple of hundred metres ahead, they could see their target – Ripley Bridge.

'Go, go, go,' Jack shouted.

Charlie pulled out her own set of grippers and scrambled on to the roof of the train after Wren, then immediately spun back and held out her hand. Jack passed her the briefcase and she disappeared for a moment before holding out her hand again. 'Get up here.'

'It's too late.' Jack waved at the approaching bridge. 'Don't miss it.'

Charlie's eyes went wide. 'But –'

'I'll be all right. I'll find another way. Just get the case out of here.'

Charlie hesitated, then vanished again.

'Slink?' Jack said into his headset.

'I'm here.' Slink's head popped up above the bridge and three bungee cords dropped over the edge just as the train passed underneath.

Jack held his breath and looked back.

To his relief he could just about see that Charlie and Wren had hooked themselves on to the bungee cords and were now hanging below the bridge, swinging back and forth in their harnesses.

Jack let out a breath. They were safe.

Now for the next problem.

He looked ahead again.

The train started to slow as the station came into view.

'Jack,' Obi said in his ear, 'you've got company.'

Three men were standing on the platform. The one in the middle – wearing a leather jacket – stepped forward, his eyebrows knitting together as he noticed the side door to the armoured carriage was open. His gaze met Jack's. He pointed and said something to his companions.

Jack pulled back and hurried into the compartment at the end of the passenger carriage.

The conductor peered through the door at him, his face twisted into rage.

But he was the least of Jack's problems right now.

He reached inside the panel and hit the button on Charlie's circuit board.

The door to the outside opened again and he peered out to the platform as they pulled in.

The three men had drawn guns with suppressors and were waiting for him. Would they really risk shooting a kid in public?

Jack knew the answer to that was likely to be a resounding 'Yes'. The Shepherd had warned him about the types of people from whom the Outlaws were stealing the briefcase.

'Jack?' It was Slink.

'Bit busy, mate.'

'I've got an idea.'

The conductor banged his fists on the door and it flexed outward.

Jack edged away from it. 'Better make it fast.'

'You're gonna have to jump.'

Jack didn't understand what Slink was getting at. 'From the train?' he said. That was kind of a given. 'Wait.' Suddenly he got it. 'There's no way I'm doing that.'

'I've looked at it and I know it's deep enough, Jack. Trust me, it'll be fine.' Though Slink didn't sound convincing. 'We're almost there and Obi can guide you to us. We'll be in position in two minutes.'

'I'm not doing it, Slink.' Jack peered around the door again, back at the station. 'I'd rather get shot.'

The lead man stepped forward – his face twisted into a snarl.

'You'll make it, easy,' Slink said.

'Yeah,' Charlie said. 'Don't be such a wimp, Jack. There's no other way for you to get to us.'

Before the train had come to a complete halt, Jack leapt out on to the platform.

'Oi,' one of the men shouted.

Jack turned and sprinted in the opposite direction.

A muffled gunshot rang out.

Jack ducked and kept running.

He jumped off the end of the platform and raced along the tracks. 'Where is it?' he shouted into his headset as another bullet whizzed past his ear. 'Why do people always want to shoot me?' He was running as fast as he could – his arms pumping the air and his feet pounding the gravel – and was already out of breath.

'We're in position,' Charlie said. 'Obi?'

'I can see him.'

Jack glanced up at a camera mounted high on a pole, then over his shoulder at the men. All three were chasing him.

For the first time in his life, Jack wished the police would turn up.

He looked forward again and, keeping his head low, sprinted as hard as he could alongside the tracks.

A bullet thudded into a tree trunk to his right.

'You're nearly there,' Obi said. 'Ten more metres. When I say, go right, between the trees. There's a gap in the fence. OK...*now.*'

Jack darted right, between two pine trees. Ahead was a wire fence with a hole in it. He ducked through and kept running.

One of the men shouted.

Jack glanced back and saw that he was caught up in the wire.

'Keep going,' Obi said.

Jack scrambled up an embankment and at the top he stopped. 'Where are you?' Ahead was the River Thames.

'We're there,' Charlie said. 'Just do it.'

One of the men shouted again, and Jack spun back to see the three of them were now climbing the embankment towards him.

'Right,' Obi said.

Jack ran, reached a low fence and hopped over it on to a concrete path.

'Left,' Obi said.

'I know.' Jack had already seen the flight of stairs. He hurried up them and at the top sprinted along the narrow bridge.

He stopped once he'd gauged he was in the middle and cursed to himself as he climbed up on to the railing. The bridge was at least ten metres above the river.

'You're doing great,' Obi said.

'Easy for you to say – you're back at the bunker, watching this on TV.'

'Kid,' said a deep voice.

Jack glanced to his left. The three men were walking slowly towards him and the lead one had lowered his gun.

'Give us the briefcase.'

'I haven't got it,' Jack said.

The man hesitated. 'Where is it?'

'I'll show you.' Jack looked forward and sucked in a deep breath.

The lead man stepped forward. 'Don't you da–'

Jack closed his eyes and jumped.

CHAPTER TWO

AS HE FELL, JACK MADE HIS BODY GO RIGID, crossed his arms over his chest and pointed his toes straight down.

He hit the water hard and the shock of the cold made him expel all the air from his lungs. Jack opened his eyes and was greeted by a foggy green haze.

Regaining his senses, he struggled towards the light above him, clawing for the surface and finally punching through, gasping for air.

The three men stared down from the bridge. They seemed as surprised as Jack was that he was still alive.

Jack trod water, looking around.

Where were they?

Suddenly, to his left, a miniature submarine cut through the water, heading straight for him.

Stingray. Jack had never thought he'd be so glad to see the metal death trap.

The top hatch opened and Wren stuck her head out. 'Quick,' she said, beckoning him over.

Jack swam to her and hauled himself on board. He climbed into the coning tower, gave the men on the bridge a quick wave, then ducked inside and closed the hatch above him.

Once safely on the seat, he looked around. Wren was sitting behind him. Charlie was at the controls in front.

'Where's Slink?'

'He stayed topside to make sure you were OK.' Charlie handed him a towel. 'We're meeting him at a rendezvous point.' Charlie pushed forward on the controls – 'Diving' – and Stingray nosed down.

'Hey, Jack?' came Slink's voice in his ear.

'Yeah?'

'I just want to say, that was freakin awesome. I recorded it on my shoulder cam. Might put it on YouTube later.'

'Don't you dare,' Jack muttered as he hugged himself and shivered.

• • •

An hour later, Jack, Charlie, Slink and Wren made their way along the tunnels under London – through the abandoned station via Badbury platform, down in the rickety lift and finally into the airlock corridor.

Charlie typed a code into the glowing blue keypad. The airlock door hissed open and the four of them walked into the main bunker.

Obi was sitting in his modified dentist's chair, surrounded by screens. 'That was a close one.'

'You're telling me.' Jack strode to the bathroom, yanked a fresh towel off the radiator and hurried to his room to get changed.

A few minutes later, he returned to the group as Charlie set the briefcase down on the dining table.

'Well,' she said, 'that mission was a lot of hassle. I hope it was worth it.'

Slink opened the fridge, took out several cans of lemonade and chucked one to each of them.

'Hey, Charlie.' Jack stared at the briefcase. 'Can you open the lock without breaking it, or showing any signs that it's been messed with?'

'No problem,' she said, taking a sip of her drink. 'Why?'

'I think we should find out what's in it.'

'Thank God for that,' Slink said. 'It's been driving me crazy not knowing what's in there.'

'Me too,' Wren said. 'It could be a bomb.'

'It's not a bomb,' Obi said. 'If it was, the way you guys shook it about getting it here, it would've exploded by now.'

'He has a point.' Charlie lifted the case off the table and marched down the corridor to her workshop.

Jack went over to Obi. 'Any sign of Hector?'

Hector's real name was Quentin Del Sarto and Obi had been monitoring forums, emails and electronic messages, keeping an eye out for him.

'He hasn't surfaced,' Obi said. 'Your program only transmitted his location that one time.' He brought up a map of America on the main screen – 'Here' – and zoomed in on New York.

Jack nodded. 'What about his dad?'

The Outlaws had found out that Benito Del Sarto was not dead but in a coma. So far they'd been unable to locate which hospital he was in.

'No luck there either,' Obi said.

Jack let out a breath. 'So there's definitely no other way – we have to get to America and track Hector down.'

Obi looked at Jack. 'That still leaves us the problem of tracing him once we get there.'

'I know,' Jack said. 'One thing at a time.' Besides, he was hoping that being a few thousand miles away would make Hector feel safe. 'I'm off to see how Charlie's getting on. Let us know if you find anything on either of the Del Sartos.'

'Will do.'

Jack strode down the corridor, turned left at the end, then took a right. Charlie's workshop was ten feet wide and thirty long. On each side were benches running the length of the room. They were filled with electronics in various states of being taken apart – TVs, games consoles, media players, digital radios – and hundreds of tools, ranging from tiny screwdrivers to huge welding machines with gas tanks.

Charlie was sitting at a desk at the end of the room.

As Jack walked towards her, there was a loud beeping sound that made him jump. 'What the –?'

Charlie turned in her chair and grinned. She pointed at the wall. There was a laser mounted to a circuit board with a speaker above it. 'I fitted that yesterday,' she said. 'It's to stop you creeping up on me.'

Jack frowned. 'I do *not* creep.' He dropped into the chair next to her and looked at the briefcase. 'Any luck?'

'I was about to call you.' She pressed the tabs, releasing the locks.

'Wait, wait, wait,' Slink shouted from the door. He marched over to join them. 'I hope you weren't about to open that without us.'

Charlie rolled her eyes. 'We would've told you what's inside.'

Slink made a tutting sound. 'Sure you would.' He scooped the briefcase from the desk and strode back towards the door.

'Where are you going with that?' Jack said.

'Wren and Obi want to see what's in it too.' Slink shook his head. 'And you're always telling us we're a team, Jack.'

Jack and Charlie hurried after Slink as he headed back into the main bunker.

Slink set the briefcase down on the dining room table and glanced at each of them in turn. 'Ready?'

Everyone nodded.

He opened the briefcase and frowned.

'What's in there?' Wren said, peering around the lid to see.

Slink reached inside and pulled out a velvet bag. He held it up and hefted the weight. 'It's heavy.' He undid the drawstring, opened the top of the bag and pulled the object out. His eyes went wide. In his hand was a huge diamond, as big as his fist.

It sent a million spots of light dancing around the room.

Everyone stared, mesmerised.

'Mine,' Wren said.

'No chance,' Jack said. 'We need it.'

'But we could buy our own plane with that,' Slink said. 'We wouldn't need tickets.'

'Yeah,' Obi said. 'But there's no way we're letting you fly it.'

'We're not buying a plane.' Charlie held out her hand to Slink. 'Can I see it?'

With obvious reluctance, Slink handed it to her.

Charlie examined the diamond and then pulled a phone from her pocket. She typed and scrolled for a few seconds, while muttering under her breath. Finally she said, 'I've got it.' She held up her phone so they could all see the screen. It showed a picture of the diamond on a velvet pillow. 'It's called the Alexandra Diamond – just over forty carats.'

'What's that mean?' Wren said.

'It means it's worth millions,' Slink said in awe. 'Maybe billions.'

'It's stolen,' Charlie said. 'According to this, it was nicked from a private collector over a year ago.'

'He might not realise it's gone,' Slink said, his eyes still transfixed by the diamond.

Charlie snorted. 'Sure.'

Jack took the diamond from her and slipped it back into the bag. This seemed to break the spell it had cast on everyone. 'We'd better take it to the Shepherd before he thinks we're keeping it for ourselves.'

'Jack...' Charlie watched him tighten the draw-strings. 'I'm not comfortable with this.'

'With what?' he said.

'Well, you know me.' Charlie glanced round at the others. 'I'm all for pinching stolen goods from bad guys, especially when they're so shiny, but are you sure we shouldn't hand this over to the police?'

'Are you nuts?' Slink said. He clicked his fingers. 'I've got it – we should break it up into little diamonds and sell them instead. It makes it easier to shift.' He made as if to walk to Charlie's workshop. 'I'll get a hammer.'

Wren looked shocked. 'Break it?'

Jack shook his head. 'Slink, we're not doing that.'

Slink grinned.

Jack turned back to Charlie. 'We don't have a choice right now. We have to take it to the Shepherd.' He eyed the briefcase. 'Wait – can you fit that with a tracker or something?'

'Yeah, but why – ?' A smile spread across Charlie's face as she seemed to grasp what he had in mind. 'OK, I'll get on it.'

'Thanks. But you'll need to be quick,' Jack said. 'We have to leave in thirty minutes.'

Charlie grabbed the briefcase and ran down the corridor to her workshop.

'Still reckon we should keep it,' Slink muttered.

• • •

Jack and Charlie walked through the main entrance to the British Library, a mostly red-brick building, with angled roofs and hundreds of windows.

Jack checked his phone. 'OK, this way.'

Two men stood guard either side of a door that led to a reading room.

One of them held up a hand. 'Off limits.'

'We're here to see the Shepherd,' Jack said.

The men exchanged a glance. Then one of them stepped forward. 'Arms up, sunshine.'

Jack raised his hands above his head and the man patted him down.

Satisfied Jack wasn't armed, the guard checked Charlie then stood back and opened the door.

The reading room wasn't large, and in the centre was a desk and four chairs.

On the other side of the desk was a man in a tailored pinstripe suit. He had a clean-shaven, narrow face and neat red hair, parted on the side.

He smiled as Jack and Charlie entered, but it didn't reach his eyes – his overall expression was as blank as a poker player's.

One of the men went to step inside, but the Shepherd waved him off.

As soon as the door closed, he looked at Jack. 'You must be Achilles.' The Shepherd had a posh voice, as though he worked for the Queen. His gaze moved to Charlie. 'And this must be...Pandora?'

Charlie nodded and the pair of them sat opposite him.

The Shepherd adjusted his tie. 'I've heard that you succeeded in your mission.' He held out a hand. 'May I?'

Jack put the briefcase on the table and slid it across to him.

The Shepherd rested his hands on top. 'Do you know the combination to the lock?'

Jack shook his head.

Nice try, but he wasn't stupid enough to fall for that.

The Shepherd set the code, undid the clasps, removed the velvet bag and slid out the diamond. He held it up to the light. 'Breathtaking.' After a few moments he glanced at Jack and Charlie. 'Don't you think so?'

Jack shrugged. 'We try not to think.'

'How very wise of you.' The Shepherd slid the diamond back into the bag, put it inside the briefcase and fastened the clasps again. Finally he took a breath and looked from Jack to Charlie. 'Was the mission easy? Any problems I should know about?'

'No problems,' Jack said.

'Well done. In that case . . .' he reached under his jacket, pulled out a yellow envelope and placed it on the desk in front of them, 'your payment.' With an index finger, he slid the envelope towards Jack.

Jack opened it and frowned. 'Where are the tickets?'

'Tickets?' The Shepherd leant back in his chair. 'No tickets, dear boy. You're children. And you have no passports. How else did you expect to get to New York?'

Jack glanced at Charlie – she too looked puzzled. He reached into the envelope and pulled out a napkin. It had a map scrawled on one side in black felt-tip. It seemed to be of some buildings sur-rounded by a fence. A green pen line wove in and out of them.

In the top right corner of the napkin was written a time: 9 p.m.

'Can you explain what this is?' Jack asked.

The Shepherd adjusted his cufflinks. 'That is a – crude, I grant you – map of RAF Hillgate: a military airport. You need to be there tonight, at the time indicated.' He leant forward and gestured to the envelope. 'You will also need all the items in there to help you gain entry.' The Shepherd took a breath. 'There is a sheet with instructions, explaining what you have to do. I suggest you follow them extremely carefully.' He leant back again. 'Lastly, at the top of that sheet is the time and address where your con-tact in America can pick you up.'

Jack slid the napkin back into the envelope and had the distinct feeling that any more questions wouldn't be answered.

The Shepherd held out his hand. 'Now, the other thing I asked for...'

Jack pulled a piece of paper from his pocket. He had written each of the Urban Outlaw's body weights on it. Obi had almost refused to get on the scales and only did so when Charlie asked him nicely.

Jack handed the note to the Shepherd, who examined it, then nodded. 'You are not to take anything else with you. No bags, no electronic devices, not so much as a chocolate bar, understood?'

'Why not?' Charlie said.

The Shepherd straightened his tie. 'Let's just say that any extra weight will be noticed.'

Jack stuffed the envelope into his jacket pocket. 'How do we get home again?'

'Ah, yes,' the Shepherd said, 'the return flight.' He didn't produce another envelope, but stared back at them. 'Notify me when you want to come home, and your contact in America can simply drop you back at the same address they picked you up from.'

'Someone will sneak us in?' Jack said.

The Shepherd gave him a curt nod.

'This looks too dangerous,' Charlie said, folding her arms. 'We're taking all the risk again.'

The Shepherd's eyebrows rose. 'What?' he said, looking at them both. 'You think I could just give you a set of plane tickets and you'd be on your merry way?' He played with his cufflinks and looked bored with their company. 'Follow the instructions. There are no guarantees. Like I said – you are children. The chances of your being caught are high.'

'If you really thought that,' Charlie said, interrupting him, 'you wouldn't have got us to steal that diamond.'

The Shepherd fixed them with an icy stare and interlaced his fingers. 'So, all clear?'

'Yeah,' Jack muttered. 'Clear.'

Besides, he thought, *what choice do we have?*

The Shepherd gestured to the door. 'You may go.'

Jack and Charlie stood up.

'Oh, one other thing.' The Shepherd's expression looked stern now, leaving no doubt that he was serious. 'If you get caught, I will have you killed before it leads back to me, understood?'

Nothing new there, Jack thought. Someone was always threatening them. *Just another normal day for the Urban Outlaws*.

• • •

Back at the bunker, Jack sat at the dining table. He upended the envelope the Shepherd had given them and shook it. Apart from the map drawn on the napkin and the instructions, there was a receipt with a four-digit number written in biro, a picture of a shipping container and a rusty key.

Jack sighed. 'Brilliant.'

He copied the address at the top of the sheet of instructions to his phone and hit Send.

Finally he sat back and considered that this could be some kind of stupid joke by the Shepherd. After all, now he had the diamond, he could just vanish.

They had to be on guard from here on in, looking out for any sign that they'd been duped.

Noble – their mentor – had offered to get the Outlaws a set of fake passports, but it would've taken weeks. They simply didn't have that much time.

The airlock door hissed open and Charlie, Obi and Wren walked through.

Jack had been so engrossed in his own thoughts that he hadn't even noticed they were gone. 'Where've you lot been?'

'Fitting cameras,' Obi said.

'What's wrong with the one in the airlock corridor?'

'Nothing. We just needed more.'

Jack frowned at him. 'But we're the only ones who ever come down here. No one else knows about the bunker.'

'I'm not leaving this place without an extra layer of security.'

Jack nodded. 'OK. Fair point.'

Obi walked over to his chair, climbed into it and checked the images on the screens.

Charlie sat opposite Jack at the dining table. 'We've fitted two more cameras in each corridor leading to the airlock,' she said.

'I'm setting the security to lock down the doors if the cameras detect any movement,' Obi said.

'What about rats?' Wren handed round lemonade. 'Won't they trigger it?'

'It's all right.' Obi clicked the trackerball in his armrest. 'I'm adjusting the sensitivity.'

'Right,' Jack said. 'And how do we disarm it again once we're home?'

Obi held up a small tablet computer. 'With this.' It showed the views from the three cameras guarding the bunker. Obi clicked the tablet screen and brought up a custom application. 'I can access our entire security system through this.'

'We can't take that with us,' Jack said. 'The Shepherd told us not to carry anything.'

Obi stared at him for a moment, incredulous. 'Well, that's that.' He turned off the tablet and slid it down the side of his chair. 'I'm not going.'

Jack let out a slow breath. 'Come on, Obi. We need you. Just set the automatic detection, like you said. We'll find a way to access the bunker's systems once we're back.' He refocused on the objects in front of him.

Charlie frowned. 'Well?' she said. 'What's the verdict?'

Jack slid the sheet of instructions over to her.

Charlie stared at the paper for over a minute, then looked up at him. 'Is this for real?'

Jack shrugged. 'Guess so. I've passed our arrival details on to Noble.'

'We're really gonna do it his way? Isn't that a little risky?'

'Right now it's our only option,' Jack said. 'We don't have time to do our own recon of RAF Hillgate.'

'Can we trust the Shepherd though?' Wren said.

Jack glanced at her. 'We don't have much choice.'

Charlie raised an eyebrow. 'We always have a choice, Jack. Life's full of them.' She sighed and looked at the objects laid out in front of them. 'This has got to be the weirdest deal we've ever done.'

Jack had to agree with that.

'Guys, there's a message from Slink on the system.' Obi pointed at one of the displays.

Jack said to Charlie, 'Where is he?'

'I don't know. I thought he was in his room.'

They stood and went over to Obi's chair.

Jack quickly scanned the message. 'Oh, no.'

'What's wrong?' Wren said.

Jack squeezed his eyes closed. 'Slink's not coming to America with us.'

CHAPTER THREE

JACK AND CHARLIE STOOD OUTSIDE TAYLOR House in Edmonton – a care home for the disabled and elderly. A sign on the front gate said it was due to be demolished to make way for a new housing development.

Jack turned slowly to Charlie, his eyes wide.

She had the same worried expression on her face. 'Demolition?' she said in a quiet voice. 'Why didn't Slink tell us?'

Jack shrugged. 'Didn't want to worry us.'

Slink's mum had multiple sclerosis and had been in this particular care home for just over a year.

'Come on.' Jack opened the gate and followed Charlie up the path and round the side of the house.

The back garden was at least thirty metres long and full of apple trees, winding paths and various benches scattered about. Jack and Charlie sat on the nearest one, under the shade of an immense oak.

Charlie pulled a phone from her pocket and sent a text.

'Slink?' Jack asked.

She nodded.

Jack held out a hand. 'Can I borrow that for a second? I have an idea.'

Charlie handed him the phone and Jack sent another text message. As he passed it back to Charlie, the phone beeped.

She glanced at the display. 'Slink says he'll be down in a bit.'

Five minutes later the back door opened and Slink strode over to them. 'What are you two doing here?' he said. 'You can't make me change my mind. I'm not going.' He glanced back at a window on the second floor. 'You'll have to do without me this time. I'm sorry.'

Jack gestured to the bench next to him. 'What's going on? We saw the sign out front.'

Slink sighed and sat down. 'They're on about moving her to another home because they're tearing this place down.'

'I'm sorry, Slink,' Charlie said. 'She's only just started to feel settled here, right?'

He nodded.

'Where are they moving her to?'

Slink shrugged. 'I don't know yet. That's why I have to be here. I can't let them send her to some grotty place. It has to be nice, like this one.'

He visited his mum every couple of days and made sure she was well looked after by the nurses and carers.

Every time one of the Outlaws' missions made money, they set some aside for Slink to give her.

After a few moments of silence, Jack said, 'Why didn't you tell us earlier? We could've tried to help.'

Mind you, they were almost out of funds. They couldn't even afford to do any RAKing.

'We've got other problems right now,' Slink said in a quiet voice. 'I didn't want to add to them.'

Jack glanced at Charlie. *Hector*, he thought.

'It's OK, Jack,' Slink said, seeming to notice his expression. 'I know we've got more important missions to do.'

Jack stared at him. 'No. No, we haven't. Other things, yeah, but you're far more important. You're part of our family, Slink. And so is your mum.'

'There's nothing more important than that,' Charlie added.

Jack gazed up at the window that Slink had been watching. 'When are they planning to move her?'

'I dunno,' Slink said, sounding deflated. 'The nurses reckon it'll be this month. They're finding new homes for everyone. It's chaos in there.' He sighed. 'They can't guarantee anything at the moment.'

'I'm sorry, Slink.' Jack rested a hand on his shoulder. 'We'll do everything we can to help.'

Slink looked up at the window again. 'She doesn't have any other visitors, and we don't know how long we'll be away for. I'm not sure I can take that risk, you know?'

Jack nodded. 'I understand. I've arranged for some extra help too.'

Slink frowned. 'Who from?'

Jack pointed down the side of the house as a figure approached.

Noble walked across the lawn towards them. He had dark skin, silver hair tied back into a ponytail and his long grey coat billowed in the breeze. 'Good afternoon.' He smiled at the three of them in turn. 'Glorious day.'

'Hey, Noble,' Charlie said, smiling back at him.

'Are you OK?' Noble asked Slink. 'I see they're demolishing this place. Such a shame.' He glanced around. 'It's peaceful here.' He looked at Slink. 'So, Jack said that you might need my help?'

'Mum's got nowhere to go.'

Noble bowed his head at Slink. 'I will do what I can to ease the process of finding a new home for your mother, if you'd like me to?'

'She doesn't have any money,' Slink said. 'She can't afford to go anywhere nice. Gotta be all on the Health Service thing.'

Noble nodded. 'Yes, I understand. I'm sure we can find somewhere suitable. Leave it with me.'

Slink glanced up at the window, then at Jack. 'If I came to America and something happened here, could you promise that I'd be able to come home again straight away?'

'I would do everything I could. If you needed to come back, we'd find a way.'

Slink looked at Noble. 'And you'll keep me updated if anything changes?'

Noble nodded. 'Of course.'

Slink sighed. 'OK.'

'Wait,' Charlie said. 'You're coming with us?'

'Yeah, I'm coming. You lot would probably mess it all up if I'm not there. I've bailed you out so many times I've lost count.'

'All right,' Charlie said, laughing. 'Don't overdo it.'

Jack smiled.

'Let me say goodbye to her.' Slink went back into the building.

As they watched him go, Jack said, 'We need to help his mum in whatever ways we can.'

Noble sat on the bench next to them. 'I'll see if I can come up with a few options while you're gone. Besides, help often comes from the most unexpected places.' He winked, then said, 'By the way, I've informed my American contact of your arrival time.'

Jack and Charlie grinned at him.

Noble tipped his head back, making sure his face was in the sun, sighed and closed his eyes. 'Glorious day.'

'Hey, Jack?' It was Obi.

Jack adjusted his earpiece. 'What's up?'

'I've just received a message from the Shepherd.'

'What does he want?'

'He found the tracker you put in the briefcase, and he's not happy about it.'

Jack's stomach sank and he looked at Charlie. 'But you hid it really well.'

'I did,' she said.

'That's not all,' Obi continued. 'He also says that because of what you've done, he's no longer helping us get to America.'

• • •

Jack marched across the bunker with Charlie and Slink hard on his heels. 'Can you show me the message?' he said.

Obi brought it up and Jack leant in to read it.

He was right – the Shepherd had rescinded his offer to help them get to America.

'What do we do?' Charlie said.

Jack straightened. 'Obi, can I borrow that tablet?'

Obi reached down by his chair and handed it to him.

Jack hurried down the corridor.

'Where are you going?' Slink called.

'To try to sort this out.'

• • •

Jack's bedroom was simply furnished – with a single bed and a wardrobe. On the wall he had an Einstein clock and a picture of Bournemouth beach and pier – Jack's birthplace, though he didn't remember it.

He sat on the edge of his bed, clicked on the Cerberus chat app and dialled.

As the app rang, Jack took deep breaths, calming his racing heart. Somehow he had to convince the Shepherd to change his mind.

The app continued to ring.

Jack was about to give up and think of another way when the Shepherd suddenly answered.

The man stared, looking annoyed. He was in an office with a window behind him. Blinds obscured the view. 'What do you want?' he said in a cold yet measured voice.

'First of all,' Jack said, 'I'm sorry. We shouldn't have planted a tracker in that briefcase.'

The Shepherd considered him a moment. 'No, you should not. It was unwise.' He interlaced his fingers. 'I assume your plan was to retrieve the diamond once you returned from America?'

Jack thought about lying, but knew this man would likely see straight through it. He swallowed. 'Perhaps, but we didn't do it just to get the diamond back. We put it there to trace you. I wanted to know who we're dealing with.'

'It's a little too late for that.' The Shepherd lifted a small Japanese teacup to his mouth, sipped and set it down again. 'You're playing a dangerous game, Achilles.'

'I know.' Jack softened his voice and tried to look sincere. 'How do I put this right?'

The Shepherd eyed him. 'Don't think for one moment that I trust you.'

Jack nodded.

The feeling's mutual.

'Why is it so important you go to America?' the Shepherd asked.

Jack hesitated. He didn't want to share that piece of information, but then again, he didn't see what choice he had. He decided to pick his next words carefully. 'We want to find someone.'

The Shepherd sipped his tea and rested the cup in the palm of his hand. 'Go on.'

'I – Well, that's it.'

'Right.' The Shepherd's eyes narrowed. 'This conversation is over.' He reached for the keyboard.

'Wait,' Jack said.

The Shepherd paused and looked at him.

'We're after someone. Someone who hurt one of our friends. Someone –'

The Shepherd leant back. 'Quentin Del Sarto.'

Jack froze.

The Shepherd fixed him with a level gaze.

'How...? How do you know that?' Jack said.

The Shepherd took a long sip of his tea, then set the cup down. 'I too wanted to know with whom I was dealing. I did some digging, and a fascinating story emerged.'

'How much do you know?' Jack said with a deepening sense of dread.

'Everything. I know what you did to his father. And I know about the virus. You think he's going to use it somehow, don't you?'

Jack nodded.

There were several seconds of silence, then the Shepherd announced, 'You're going to America as planned.'

Jack let out a breath. 'Thank –'

The Shepherd held up a hand. 'You're going to America. You'll hunt down this Del Sarto boy and bring me the virus.'

Jack's chest tightened. 'I –'

'That's not all.' The Shepherd leant back in his chair. 'In order to warrant return tickets, you'll also need to do a mission for me while you're in America.'

'What kind of mission?'

'I will send you details when you're safely there.' The Shepherd rested his hands on the table. 'You complete that mission, and you'll get your tickets home. And you'll bring me the virus when you're done. Clear?'

Jack hesitated, then nodded. 'Clear.'

The Shepherd's eyes narrowed. 'You try to fool me again, I will hunt you down and put an end to your *Urban Outlaws*.' He hit a button and the display went dark.

Jack stared at the screen. 'Great,' he muttered. Now he had another enemy to deal with. As if things weren't difficult enough.

He switched off the tablet and stared at his reflection in the darkened screen, while he pondered his options.

Jack's first thought was of the others – going to America with yet another mission to complete was just too risky. Besides, there was no way he was going to bring the virus back for the Shepherd.

Everything was moving so fast that Jack hadn't had time to stop and think things through properly. Maybe he could go on his own. He had a passport; it was the other Outlaws who were the problem.

Maybe Jack could find Hector in America and slow him down enough for the others to catch up once Noble had got them fake passports.

It wouldn't be easy, but it wasn't impossible.

At least with that plan they could do it without needing the Shepherd's help.

Jack let out a puff of air and stood up.

Now he had to explain it to the others and hope they'd understand.

• • •

When Jack got back to the main bunker, Charlie, Slink and Wren were gathered around Obi's chair, staring at the main screen.

'What's wrong?' Jack said, noticing how pale they all looked.

Obi pointed a shaking finger at the display.

Jack came round and stopped dead in his tracks.

On the screen was the image of Hector standing in front of a grey wall.

'Is this live?' Jack asked Obi.

'No.' Obi pointed at the Cerberus forum logo in the corner of the display. 'It's secure. He's left a recording.' Obi swallowed. 'And you're not gonna like it, Jack.' He pressed Play.

A smug grin swept across Hector's face. 'This is a message for the Urban Outlaws.' He said their name with contempt. 'And' – his eyes narrowed – 'most importantly, *Jack*.'

Now what was Hector up to? Jack wondered.

Hector held up a file and fixed the camera with an icy stare. 'Glen Draper.'

Jack gasped and looked at the others.

They each wore a solemn expression.

'Glen Draper,' Hector continued. 'Your friend, Jack. Your *mentor*, aka Noble.' He opened the file and his eyes skimmed the first page. 'The man has an impressive résumé.' He licked a finger and flipped through the sheets, scanning each in turn. 'He's had a very active life. Caused a lot of problems for a lot of people.' Hector tutted. 'Naughty. Very naughty.' He snapped the file closed and looked at the camera again. 'It would be a shame if these crimes caught up with him.' The smile dropped from his face. 'I'm sure I could invent a few new ones too.' He paused for a long while, then said, 'So, Jack, I suggest the Outlaws forget all about me and get on with your miserable little lives.'

The image went dark.

'We have to tell Noble,' Charlie said.

'No,' Jack said.

'What do you mean, no?' Charlie waved a finger at the display. 'He has to know about this.'

'If we tell him,' Jack said slowly, 'what do you think will happen?'

They all looked thoughtful a moment, then Obi said, 'Noble will do something about it. He'll go after Hector.'

'Exactly,' Jack said. 'But that's not a good idea. Hector has obviously managed to take apart the virus. We were too slow. Now he's got a customised program to hack anything he wants. He has exactly what his father wanted – the ultimate hacking tool – and we need to be extra careful. That also means tracking down Hector without Noble's help.' Jack started pacing the bunker, trying to work out what Hector's next move would be.

'But that's not the whole story. The reason Hector has gone after Noble is because even if he blamed a load of hacking on us, so what? Who cares? We're always running from the police anyway. We've done loads of stuff that could get us into trouble. Noble, on the other hand, works for lots of legitimate companies now and if Hector sets him up he'll lose everything he's worked for. We can't let that happen.' He stopped and looked at them. 'Right?'

Charlie nodded. 'What's his plan then?'

'He's trying to force us to defend Noble. He's set a trap.'

'So what?' Slink said.

'So, Hector's expecting us to go after him, but he thinks he's safe in America, remember?'

'We still carry on as planned though, right?' Obi said. 'We're still going to New York?'

Jack sighed and looked at the screen. 'We don't have a choice.'

• • •

RAF Hillgate was a Royal Air Force base just outside London. That night, Jack, Charlie, Obi, Slink and Wren sat on a hill overlooking the main runway. Several cargo planes were parked next to hangars and the whole place was alive with activity.

Jack checked he had all the stuff the Shepherd had given them and he read the instructions one last time, making sure he'd remembered them correctly. Satisfied he had, Jack consulted the map on the back of the napkin. It was crude, but did appear to match up with some of the buildings inside the compound. 'We'd better get in position,' he said, looking at his phone. It was almost nine o'clock and the instructions were specific on timings.

'And you're absolutely sure we can trust this Shepherd guy?' Slink said.

'Nope.' Jack took a deep breath and whispered to the others, 'Stay close to me. All right?'

They nodded.

He got to his feet and walked into the trees, with everyone else following. At the bottom of the hill, they continued along a narrow path that wound through the forest. At the end, exactly as the instructions had indicated, was a metal gate in a chain-link fence.

Jack pulled the rusty key from his pocket and tried it in the lock.

It worked.

He opened the gate and looked around. Mounted high on several poles he could see security cameras. He checked the map on the napkin and realised the drawn path would get them past the cameras without being spotted.

'Right,' he said, glancing at the others, 'let's go, and stay close – there's no margin of error here.'

Charlie grabbed his arm.

'What's wrong?'

She held out a hand. 'Your phone. He said we couldn't take anything.'

Jack pulled the phone from his pocket and handed it to her.

Charlie took out the battery and tossed it one way and the phone the other into the bushes.

Jack stepped through the gate and checked no one was around.

Then, following the layout on the map, they kept close to the fence until they reached an electrical box. They hid behind it as two military police officers walked past.

When they were gone, Jack and the other Outlaws hurried to a small building, darted left and stopped at a side door.

Charlie examined the electronic lock. 'Without tools, I have no chance of getting through this.'

'You don't need to.' Jack pulled the receipt out of his pocket and flipped it over. On the back were the numbers 7281. He handed it to Charlie.

She typed in the code. A red LED flashed, then turned green.

The lock clicked.

Jack squinted at the map in the dim light. The path from here on was straightforward.

He opened the door, peered inside, then gestured for Charlie and the others to go in.

With a quick glance around to make sure no one had seen them, Jack followed them through.

They were now standing in a wide corridor.

'No cameras that I can see,' Charlie whispered.

Jack nodded and listened, but all was quiet. 'Come on. This way.'

He opened the last door on the right and peered inside.

It was a supply room. Coats hung in neat rows, along with boots, gloves, shirts and various military uniforms.

Jack strode to a door at the far end, opened it and peered through.

On the other side was a huge hangar.

He hid behind a stack of wooden boxes, and while he waited for the others to join him, he looked around.

In the middle of the hangar was a cargo plane. The rear ramp was down and a crewman was load-ing crates of supplies.

'That must be our flight out of here,' Jack whispered.

Charlie groaned. 'Are you serious? How are we going to get on board?'

'I reckon I can take that guy out.' Slink cricked his neck. 'There's only one of him.'

'He's twice your size and highly trained,' Charlie hissed. 'You don't stand a chance.'

Slink winked at her. 'Challenge accepted.'

'No.' Jack grabbed Slink's shoulder and peered over the crates. 'Just wait. We don't need to do anything.'

In the corner of the hangar was an office with its door open. Inside was a desk with a phone, two chairs and a clock on the wall.

Jack squinted. 'If that clock's right, then...'

The phone started to ring.

The crewman put down the box he was carrying and marched over to the office.

Jack grinned at the others as a huge sense of relief washed over him. 'See?' The Shepherd had kept his word and the plan was working.

The crewman picked up the phone and turned his back on the door.

'Go,' Jack hissed, and the five of them sprinted to the plane and up the ramp.

Inside were several large metal containers.

Jack pulled the last item from his pocket – the picture. He checked the numbers on the containers until he found the one that matched. 'This is it.'

Slink swung the handle down and opened it.

For a few seconds, everyone stared inside.

There were five metal upright beds fixed to the walls. Strapped to each bed was a harness, an oxygen tank and a mask.

'He has got to be kidding,' Charlie muttered.

They heard footfalls behind them – the crewman was returning.

'Quick,' Jack whispered.

The Outlaws stepped into the container, and as soon as Jack had helped Slink push the door closed, a red light came on inside.

Charlie examined the seal, then the door itself.

'What do you make of it?' Jack whispered.

'Whoever modified this knew what they were doing. It's airtight, the walls are insulated and…' Charlie pointed up at a small heater mounted above the door frame.

Jack nodded and motioned for them to strap themselves into their respective beds.

'We've got to fly all the way there standing up?' Obi whispered.

Jack held up a hand and turned his ear to the door. He could hear voices outside. Other crewmen must have joined the first. Did they know the Outlaws were inside the crate?

Jack braced himself, but to his relief a deep vibration started beneath his feet.

He turned to the others again. 'They're raising the ramp,' he hissed. 'Hurry.'

Just then, the unmistakable roar of the engines fired up.

Jack jabbed a finger at the beds. '*Now.*'

With obvious reluctance, Obi, Wren and Slink strapped themselves in.

Charlie was still examining the door to the crate.

'What's wrong?' Jack whispered.

'There's no way to open this from the inside,' she said, running her fingers along the seal. She stepped back. 'We're trapped in here.'

The floor lurched and Jack and Charlie staggered backwards.

'Too late. We're moving.' Jack helped secure Charlie into her upright bed then strapped himself into his own.

The bed was surprisingly comfortable. Well, for now at least. Part of the padded straps went under his arms and held his shoulders back.

How long would the flight take? Jack thought. Six hours? Ten? Longer?

After a few minutes, the plane turned sharply to the right and came to a sudden halt.

Charlie lowered her mask. 'Runway,' she mouthed.

Jack nodded and glanced at the others. Obi and Wren looked panicked, but Slink seemed positively excited.

Jack pulled the oxygen mask over his face and tried to pretend he was somewhere else, not about to be propelled thousands of feet into the air.

The engines roared, vibrating the metal container around them, and the plane lunged forward.

Green lights flicked on above each of the oxygen tanks and there was a hissing sound as their masks filled.

Jack took deep breaths, allowing air to fill his lungs.

Suddenly a strange tingling sensation came over him. He looked over at the others. Slink was frowning at his hands and flexing them.

Wren's eyes closed and she slumped forward in her harness. A second later, so did Obi.

Jack's vision started to blur. He tried to reach up to his mask, but he couldn't – no matter what signals he tried to send to his arms, they just stayed limp by his sides.

Jack watched helplessly as Charlie and Slink passed out too, and before he had time to really panic, his world turned to darkness.

CHAPTER FOUR

JACK HEARD THE FAINT RHYTHM OF HIS OWN breathing.

I'm alive, he thought, with detached relief.

Groggy, he tried to open his eyes, but he couldn't – his eyelids felt as though they were filled with lead.

There was a rumbling engine noise, this one quieter than the plane's. There was a *thunk* against one side of the container and Jack felt them lurch backwards.

They bumped along, and after another minute or so the container tipped forward again and this was followed by a scraping sound.

Lorry, he thought. Someone had loaded the container on to a lorry and was now taking them to the rendezvous point.

Or so he hoped.

Jack felt a hint of panic as he vaguely wondered whether everything had gone to plan.

Were they in America? They could be in any country in the world for all he knew.

Before he could think any more about it, blackness engulfed him again.

• • •

Warm red light cut through the darkness, and this time Jack felt his body slowly come back to life.

Keeping his eyes closed, he flexed each muscle in turn, mentally checking each limb off: feet, legs, hands, arms, shoulders...As far as he could tell, all seemed to be intact and working.

Finally Jack managed to open his eyes and he blinked a few times.

Charlie, Obi, Slink and Wren were still in their harnesses, strapped to their upright beds, and were waking up too.

Jack shook off the remaining grogginess and looked at the door to the container. It was closed, but there was no sound of engines or movement on the other side of it.

For a few minutes, everyone was still, listening.

Suddenly there was clattering and a heavy grinding noise, followed by the sound of an engine, but one less powerful than before – a car perhaps?

Jack signalled to the others and they all released their harnesses and stepped from the upright beds.

He glanced at the container door, then at Charlie. 'What do you think?' he whispered.

'Nothing we can do,' she whispered back. 'We can't get out of here until someone opens it from the other side.'

Jack assumed their compartment had been deliberately designed that way.

Slink cricked his neck and bounced lightly on the balls of his feet. Then he hunched down, ready to pounce.

The engine noise stopped and a car door opened and closed.

Jack motioned for Obi and Wren to hang back while he and Charlie stood either side of the container's door.

Footfall approached and the Outlaws braced themselves.

The door opened and Jack squinted.

Standing in the light was a tall dark woman with long hair. She wore a leather jacket, jeans and a blue T-shirt.

'*Serene*.' Charlie leapt forward.

They embraced for a moment, then Serene smiled at them all. 'I'm so happy you made it here OK.' Her American accent was softened by her time spent in England. 'When I heard where we had to meet, I was worried.'

Slink straightened up from his crouch. 'Hey, Serene.'

'Slink.' She hugged him. 'You must be at least six inches taller than last time I saw you.'

'Hi, Serene,' Obi said.

Serene gave him a hug too. Then her eyes moved to the youngest of their group. 'And this must be Wren?'

'Hi.' Wren thrust out a hand and they shook.

Serene smiled at her. 'I've heard a lot about you.' She glanced between them all. 'Noble keeps me updated on everything you Outlaws get up to.' She looked at Jack and winked.

Serene was Noble's sister and you could see the family resemblance – especially in the eyes. During her time in the UK, Serene had helped out with some of the Outlaw's missions and had taught Charlie everything about electronics and building gadgets.

Charlie often said that she'd be useless without Serene's teachings, but Jack couldn't imagine

Charlie being useless at anything. She had a natural gift at understanding how things worked.

Jack peered out of the container. They were in some kind of giant warehouse. Hundreds of other containers were all around, stacked and packed into rows.

Serene stepped aside and gestured to a laundry van parked by the main roller door. 'I think we should get out of here, don't you?'

The Outlaws hurried from the container over to the van, where Serene opened the back doors. 'You'll need to hide until we're well away from this place.'

Inside the back of the van were piles of laundry bags, bed linen and towels.

'In you go. They're all clean,' Serene said, eyeing Wren's look of disgust.

The Outlaws clambered in and pulled sheets and towels over themselves.

• • •

Twenty minutes later, and once Serene was sure it was safe for them to come out of hiding, they pulled the sheets and towels off their heads and peered out of the van's rear windows.

Jack caught glimpses of New York City as they drove over a bridge.

It was mesmerising, and even though he'd seen pictures, he hadn't expected it to look quite so big. Some of the buildings in London were impressive, but this was something else – hundreds of concrete and glass skyscrapers all crammed together.

• • •

After travelling through what seemed like half of New York, Serene wound her way along a set of narrow streets.

Wren stared out of the window, her eyes wide. 'Where are we now?'

'Chinatown.' Serene turned a corner.

Pell Street was crammed full of shops, restaurants and hair salons. Signs in Chinese hung everywhere, competing for attention.

Serene parked the van and the six of them clambered out. 'This way.'

They walked into a narrow shop.

The walls were lined with hundreds of shoes and boots in neat rows.

An ancient Chinese woman stood behind a counter. She bowed as Serene led the way through a door at the back of the shop and into a storeroom full of shoeboxes.

On the far wall she opened another door, and beyond that was a spiral staircase. The six of them hurried up, twisting skyward until they suddenly found themselves in a huge open loft space.

With its high ceiling and polished wooden flooring, it was a stark contrast to the crowded shoe shop.

The loft was about the same size as the main area of the Outlaws' bunker, only it was bright because of the large windows.

To the right was a sitting area with black leather sofas and chairs. Next to them was a set of glass doors that led to a garden terrace.

On the left-hand side of the staircase was a kitchen, and opposite that an office with a desk, chair and server cabinets.

Jack's attention was drawn to the end of the room – the entire wall was made of glass.

Charlie moved slowly towards it, her eyes wide, her mouth hanging open.

Behind the glass was a brightly lit area with lots of cabinets and shelves.

Serene smiled as she noticed Charlie's expression. 'My gadget room,' she said. 'Would you like a closer look?'

Charlie nodded.

Serene glanced at the others. 'Help yourself to food and drinks, and make yourselves comfortable.'

'Can I call my mum?' Slink asked.

'Of course.' Serene pointed to a phone on the wall. 'Help yourself.' She strode to the glass door of the gadget room and held it open.

Jack and Charlie walked through.

They peered inside the glass cabinets and examined the objects on the shelves.

In the first cabinet was recording equipment and cameras of various sizes and shapes – some disguised to look like smoke detectors, pens and other household items.

Another cabinet was filled with tracking devices, while the one next to it had remote-controlled helicopters like Shadow Bee and an object half a metre across with rotor blades in each of its four corners and a camera in the middle.

'What's that?' Jack said.

'A drone.' Charlie was practically salivating. She moved on and stared at a set of night-vision goggles.

Jack walked to the back wall, where several bulletproof vests hung from hooks. 'Do you need to wear those much?' he asked Serene.

She inclined her head. 'You can't be too careful.'

He stopped in front of a strange suit made from metal rods, motors and pistons. 'And that?'

'Exoskeleton,' Serene said. 'Haven't used that one yet.' She looked over at Charlie. 'So, what do you think?'

Charlie's eyes were wide and she seemed like she'd reached heaven. 'It's amazing.'

'I'm not as clever as you,' Serene said. 'I have to *buy* my gadgets.' She smiled.

Charlie glanced at Jack. 'My stuff doesn't always work.'

'Works most of the time.' Jack gestured to a large crate – two metres long, one metre wide – sitting in a corner of the room. 'What's in there?'

'Ah, yes, you'll like this.' Serene strode over to the crate and lifted up the lid. 'See for yourself.'

Lying inside, secured with thick straps, was a large cylinder jutting out of a metal box. It reminded Jack of a cannon.

He frowned. 'What is that?'

'It's a secret military prototype called the "Stinger",' Serene said. 'It fires two hardened prongs hundreds of metres.' She pointed at the back of it. 'In there are two spools of wire.'

Charlie frowned. 'Really? What's it for?'

'They were experimenting on enemy tanks and other vehicles. Using the Stinger to fry their electronics.'

'How did you get hold of it?' Jack asked.

Serene gave him a sly smile. 'Someone owed me a favour. A very *big* favour.' She shut the lid and went over to a bench on the opposite side of the room. 'I have this set up for you, Charlie, should you need it.' She pressed a button and plug sockets rose from hidden compartments as Serene turned to a cupboard and opened it.

Inside was a soldering iron, various thicknesses of cable on reels and a full set of tools. Everything Charlie might need to make one of her custom gadgets.

Jack had never seen Charlie look so excited and stunned all at the same time.

Next to the cupboard was a 3D printer.

'That's awesome,' Charlie said.

Jack could almost see the cogs in her brain churning over with the million ideas she had for it.

'And this is called a Think Desk.' Serene waved her hand and an interface appeared in one corner. 'It's an interactive workstation. I use this to examine items and create mind maps.'

'I've seen one of those on the internet.' Jack let out a puff of air. Serene's gadget room must have cost her millions.

Serene waved her hand again and the Think Desk turned off. 'Now, you must be starving.'

• • •

An hour later and their stomachs were all full. Serene had prepared homemade hamburgers and French fries, followed by chocolate ice cream.

Obi, Wren and Slink had two helpings of everything to make up for the lack of food during their flight.

Serene explained that she had bought them all toiletries and several changes of clothes, which they would find in the linen cupboard. Also, there were five camping mattresses rolled up under the sofas in the seating area.

She had thought of everything.

'I need to warn you that I will have to go away at short notice. Could be in the next day or so.'

Jack nodded. 'OK.'

'I'm sorry, but it's an important mission and I can't get out of it.'

'What are you doing?' Wren said.

Charlie shot her a look. 'You can't ask something like that. It's private.'

'It's OK.' Serene smiled at Wren. 'Let's just say a very bad man is about to get his karma delivered to him.'

Wren grinned back at her.

Once, when Serene had come over to England, the Outlaws had managed to help her out by breaking into some guy's flat and recovering a stolen phone. Though she hadn't been too forthcoming with information, Jack had later learned that the phone had belonged to a terrorist.

'That reminds me.' Serene went into her gadget room and returned a minute later carrying a strange-looking device. It was only a centimetre or so thick, about fifty centimetres square, had six buttons and a large screen.

She handed it to Wren. 'This is for you. I've heard you're good at games.'

Wren took it from her and examined the device. 'What is it?'

'It's called *Hamster Escape*. I've been trying to complete it for months.' Serene sat down. 'Ironic thing is, I actually programmed the stupid thing myself.'

Wren's eyes widened. 'You did?'

Slink huffed. 'Wren's not *that* good at games.'

Wren scowled at him. 'I beat you every time on that racing one back at the bunker.' She switched on *Hamster Escape* and started playing. After a few seconds, she looked up at Serene. 'It's awesome. Thanks.'

Serene waved her away. 'You think it's cool now – wait until you get to level seventeen.'

Jack glanced over at Serene's office. 'Can I borrow your computer?'

'You want to get to work tracking down your friend?'

Jack rose from his chair. 'Yes, please.' He strode towards the glass office door.

'The password is *Firefly*.'

'Thanks.' Jack pushed the door open and went inside.

The office was sparse – just a desk and chair against one wall. Next to the desk was a door that Jack assumed led to Serene's bedroom.

He sat down and turned in the seat to look at the servers behind him. They were humming quietly. They were the best – Ryalls Eighty-Six – no expense spared.

Jack looked at the monitor, nudged the mouse and typed in the password.

Serene had programmed her own operating system and it ran smoothly, better than he could've hoped for. The internet connection was fast, and she had also created some superb firewalls and proxies to protect her anonymity.

Jack opened a dialog box and spent the next few minutes checking the IP address of Hector's last known location. Finally he brought up a map, stood and opened the door.

'Serene?'

She strode over to him. 'Everything OK?'

'Could you help me out a minute?' Jack pointed at the screen. 'Do you know where that is?'

She nodded. 'It's an apartment building near the park. Very exclusive. Why?'

'That's where the virus is.'

Charlie, Obi, Slink and Wren came over to see what Jack had found.

'We need to do a recon mission,' Jack said.

Obi groaned. '*Now?* Can't it wait till tomorrow? I'm tired.'

'No,' Jack said. 'We have to act quickly.'

Obi's shoulders slumped.

'You're always tired,' Slink said.

'You're always annoying,' Obi mumbled back.

'And sarcastic,' Wren said with a grin.

Slink gasped. 'I am *never* sarcastic.'

Charlie turned to Jack. 'What do you want us to do?'

• • •

Charlie loaded up with gadgets she thought they might need, and thirty minutes later Jack, Charlie, Slink, Wren and Serene pulled up in the van on Fifth Avenue and 79th Street.

To their right was Central Park and to their left was a building with concrete columns, twelve storeys high.

Jack peered up at it.

'The Hindleton Building,' Serene said.

Charlie leant forward in the passenger seat. 'Hector's here?'

'Yep.' Jack looked around. 'He must have rented one of the apartments.'

'Which one?' Slink said.

Jack let out a breath. 'No idea.' He pressed a finger to his ear. Serene had lent them all a set of low-profile earpieces, connected to phones. 'Obi?'

'Commander Obi, receiving.' He was in Serene's office.

Jack fought the urge to snap at him. 'Have you got into the CCTV systems yet?'

'I have visuals from three cameras in the surrounding roads,' Obi said. 'This set-up is amazing. Took me under thirty seconds to get in. One camera is two buildings down and I can see the front of the apartments.'

'Any sign of Hector yet?'

'No. Since I've tapped in, no one has gone in or out.'

'OK. Thanks. Keep us updated.' Jack sat back, mulled over various plans for a moment, then glanced at Charlie. 'I think we should move.'

'You have a plan?' she said.

Jack nodded and turned to Wren. 'Up for playing the "little lost girl"?'

Wren beamed at him.

'I'll take that as a yes.'

'What do you want me to do?' Slink said.

'Nothing at the moment,' Jack said. 'This is just recon.'

Jack, Charlie and Wren climbed out of the van and Jack glanced up and down the street. It was busy with cars and pedestrians.

He looked across the road, at the trees and Central Park beyond. If they needed to physically watch the building without using CCTV, there were plenty of places to hide.

They walked to the front of the apartment building. The doorman's eyes narrowed as they approached, but he opened the doors for them anyway.

'Thanks,' Jack said, following Charlie and Wren inside.

The lobby was lavish, with marble floors and a crystal chandelier. A woman in a dark blue suit with gold buttons was standing behind a mahogany desk. She looked up and a frown creased her brow.

'Excuse me, miss,' Charlie said, laying the British accent on nice and thick. 'We found this girl outside.' She pointed to Wren.

Tears streamed down Wren's face and she sniffed.

The woman studied her. 'Go find a policeman in the park.'

Charlie visibly bristled at the woman's attitude, but recovered herself. 'She says she lives here.'

The woman's pencilled eyebrows rose. 'Oh, really?'

Wren nodded and wiped her nose on her sleeve.

A man in a suit and long coat walked in through the main doors.

'Good day, Mr Granger,' said the woman behind the desk.

He nodded and walked to a door to the right. Jack assumed this led to the stairs and lift.

The woman typed a code into the computer next to her and the door buzzed.

Jack glanced at the back of it, but there were no network cables that he could see – which meant it was on an isolated system.

The man pushed through the door without a backward glance.

Next, Jack scanned the walls and ceiling of the lobby, but couldn't see any signs of cameras.

The woman sighed and looked at Wren. 'What apartment number?'

'I don't know,' Wren said through heavy sobs.

'I can't help you then.' The woman waved her away.

A smartly dressed man and woman strode through the main doors.

Wren's crying burst into loud sobs.

The woman behind the desk glanced uneasily at the man and woman as they stepped to the door.

She typed in a code and they walked through. 'Right,' she said in a low voice, once they'd gone, 'what's your name?'

'Jennifer Del Sarto.'

The receptionist crossed her arms. 'Del Sarto?'

'Yeah,' Charlie said. 'She said her brother's name is Quentin.'

'Get out.'

'What?'

'The Del Sarto family have been with us for many years,' the woman snapped. 'They are our most valued tenants and I know for a fact that Master Del Sarto does not have a sister.'

'Yes, he does,' Wren said.

The woman scowled at her and picked up the phone. 'Would you like me to call the police?'

Wren instantly stopped crying. 'No.'

The woman slammed the phone down and thrust a finger at the main doors. 'Get out.'

Charlie opened her mouth to reply, but Jack took her arm.

'Come on,' he said. 'Let's go.'

Outside, Jack, Charlie and Wren hurried back to the laundry van and climbed in.

'How did you get on?' Serene said.

'Don't ask,' Charlie mumbled.

Jack looked at Slink, who was now wearing a New York Yankees baseball cap. 'Where did you get that?'

'Found it in a bag while I was waiting for you lot. Serene said I could have it. I wanna blend in with the locals.'

'Well,' Charlie said, as Serene pulled the van from the kerb, 'that was a disaster.'

'No, it wasn't,' Jack said.

Charlie frowned. 'Huh?'

'Now we know Hector is definitely staying there.'

Charlie's confusion gave way to a cheeky grin. 'You've got a new plan?'

Jack nodded. 'Yep. And this next mission is going to be a challenge.'

Slink rubbed his hands together. 'Bring it on.'

CHAPTER FIVE

IT WAS GETTING DARK BY THE TIME SERENE parked the van down a side street in Chinatown. Jack felt jet-lagged and disorientated, and his brain refused to accept what time of day it was.

The others looked tired too, and as they climbed out of the van and were about to go into the shop, someone called, 'Serene?'

A hooded figure, wearing a leather jacket with straps on the arms, gloves, black trousers and heavy leather boots with metal caps, jogged up to her.

'Lux?' Serene said. 'Is that you?'

'Yeah, it's me.' The girl pulled down her hood. She had light blonde hair, pale skin, blue eyes and several piercings – five in her right ear, four in her left and one in her nose.

Jack thought she was beautiful. He glanced at Slink, and by the look on his face, he thought so too.

Charlie noticed their gormless expressions and rolled her eyes.

Serene looked up and down the street, took Lux's arm and huddled in the doorway to the shoe shop. 'What's wrong?'

'Huge trouble.' Lux's suspicious gaze moved to the others.

'It's OK,' Serene said. 'They're with me.' She opened the door and ushered everyone through.

Once up in Serene's loft, they all slumped on the sofas.

'This is Jack, Charlie, Slink and Wren,' Serene said.

Lux nodded. 'Hi.'

The office door opened and Obi strolled through. 'Hey, guys.' He dropped a stack of papers on to the dining room table. 'I printed everything you asked for, Jack.' He flopped into a vacant space on one of the sofas. 'How was –?' Obi spotted Lux and his jaw dropped.

Charlie sighed, leant over and closed it for him. 'This is Obi. Obi, meet Lux.'

Lux smiled. 'Hi.'

Obi just stared at her.

'Lux is an expert on New York,' Serene said. 'She knows every street, every building layout. If you need help breaking in anywhere, she's the one to ask.'

'Impressive,' Jack said.

'My dad was a local historian. He had hundreds of books and plans of the city.' Lux gazed out of the window a moment. 'I memorised them all.'

'So,' Serene said, 'tell me what's going on.'

Lux looked back at her. 'I'm not sure where to begin. It started a couple hours ago.'

'What did?'

'Everyone's being set up. Kismet, Glitch...All those guys.'

'What do you mean, "set up"?' Serene said.

'Well, Kismet was first. The FBI arrested him for hacking a children's charity account and transferring ten thousand dollars to his own bank account.'

'That can't be right,' Serene said. 'Kismet would never do a thing like that. He's a good kid.'

'I know.' Lux shook her head. 'At first we couldn't understand what was going on, but then Glitch was next.'

'What about Glitch?'

'He supposedly hacked an ATM in Times Square. It completely emptied itself on to the street before the cops spotted people fighting over the money and

87

tried to stop it.' Her eyes darted to the window as a police siren sounded in the distance. 'His apartment was raided, but he managed to get out. So far he's avoided the FBI.'

'Tell him to come here,' Serene said.

'I think he's OK for now,' Lux said. 'He's gone to Harvey's place. He'll be safe there.' She let out a breath and sat back. 'Anyway, we don't know what's going on yet. Everyone's on edge.'

'We know what's happening,' Jack said. 'We've been tracking this guy called Hector. That's why we're here – we're trying to stop him.'

'This is one person?' Lux said, incredulous.

'He's created a program to hack anything he wants.' Jack stood up and started to pace the room.

'What are you thinking?' Charlie said.

'Hector's now attacking hackers, right?'

'Yeah, but why?' Wren said.

Jack stopped pacing and turned to the group. 'My guess is he's eliminating all the local threats first – anyone that could potentially track him down and reveal where he's hiding. He'll start here in New York, then move out until he's set up every hacker he finds.'

'He'll then be free to do whatever he wants,' Obi said.

'You're right,' Lux said. 'That's what I'd do if I had that kind of power.'

Obi's cheeks flushed and he looked down at his feet.

'It's actually quite clever when you think about it,' Serene said.

'Nah,' Slink said. 'The guy's an idiot, and when I get my hands on him, I'm going to kick him right in the bu–'

'*Slink*,' Charlie interrupted, frowning at him.

'Bungalow,' Wren said, laughing. 'Kick him in the bungalow, Slink.'

They both giggled like three-year-olds.

'Bungalow?' Obi said, looking thoroughly confused. 'That makes no sense.'

Serene glanced at them all in turn. 'You need to lie low for a while.'

Charlie looked shocked. 'Hide?' she said, her voice raising an octave. 'Urban Outlaws don't run from anything.'

Jack cocked an eyebrow at her. 'What are you on about? We're always running.'

Charlie crossed her arms. 'We don't back down though.'

Serene said, 'There are times in life when you have to.'

Charlie looked infuriated. 'But we need to act. We have to find Hector *now*.'

'Charlie's right,' Lux said. 'From what you say, this is only likely to get worse.'

Serene's mobile phone beeped. She looked at the display and groaned. 'I can't believe it.'

'What's wrong?' Lux said.

'I have to go. I'm so sorry.'

'Go where?' Wren said.

'That mission I told you about.' She hurried to the gadget room, walked over to a metal cabinet, opened it and pulled out a canvas bag. She strode back into the room as she checked the bag's contents. 'I shouldn't be too long. A couple of days at the most.'

'Do you need any help?' Lux said.

Serene zipped the bag up. 'I have to do this one alone.' She hurried to the spiral staircase. 'I'm so sorry I have to leave you, especially now. I'll be back as quick as I can. There's plenty of food in the cupboards.' She looked at Jack. 'I really am sorry. I have no choice.'

Jack nodded. 'It's OK. Thanks for everything.'

Serene half smiled at them all, then left.

Slink looked at Jack. 'Great, now we know where Hector is, but we have no transport.'

'Where do you need to go?' Lux said. 'If someone is setting up my friends, I want to help.'

'Fifth Avenue,' Jack said. 'There's an apartment building opposite Central Park, near 79th Street.'

Lux stood up. 'I'll call Drake.'

'Who's Drake?'

'Another friend of mine. He's our local transport expert, and when he hears what's going on, I'm sure he'll wanna help us.'

'Thanks.' Jack walked over to the dining table, spread the papers out and stared at them.

Obi had printed various plans, maps and pictures of the apartment building and surrounding area.

There had to be a way in there without being spotted, but Jack was struggling to find it.

The others quietly gathered around the table and helped.

A few minutes later, Lux joined them at the table. 'Drake says he can take us. When you're ready, I'll text him, and he'll be here in fifteen minutes.'

'That's brilliant,' Jack said. 'Thank you.'

Lux looked at the printouts. 'Can I help?'

Jack pointed at a street view of the Hindleton Building. 'I'm pretty sure Hector's apartment will be on the top floor.'

'How do you know that?' Obi said.

Jack put the picture down. 'The receptionist said the Del Sarto family were their most valued clients. That means they would have the finest apartment in the building. That'll also mean they'll have the best view over Central Park. The upper two storeys have balconies and there are four balconies per floor, which means two per apartment.' Jack held up a zoomed-in image of the top floor and pointed. 'Hector will be in one of those.'

'Right,' Charlie said. 'But how are we going to break in?'

'We can't go through the front,' Jack said. 'The doorman knows our faces and he'll probably warn his replacement when his shift finishes. Besides, even if we could get into the lobby again, the woman behind the desk has control of the inner door via her computer. There's no way to just sneak past.'

'If she controls it by a computer, can't you hack it?' Obi said.

'No,' Lux said. She looked at Jack. 'Isolated security, right?'

Jack nodded.

'So,' Charlie said, straightening up, 'the front way into the apartment is out of the question.'

'Yep.'

'What about the back?' Lux pointed. 'There's an alleyway. There must also be a back way in.'

'Yeah, I know.' Jack held up the satellite image. 'But they have isolated CCTV cameras.'

'What about this?' Slink slid over a plan of the sewers under the building.

'No way through those,' Lux said. 'The nearest pipes big enough for a person run from Central Park to a manhole in that alley.' She pointed. 'It does branch off here, under the building, but it's no good, too small.'

Obi huffed. 'Are you sure we need to go right now, Jack? Can't we wait? Take the time to plan something properly?'

Jack shook his head. 'We have to do it tonight before Hector realises we're on to him and disappears. And I need to go myself, in case we have to hack into Hector's computers or something.' He sat back and let out a defeated breath.

Everyone stared at the printouts for a long while.

Finally Slink said, 'So, that only leaves the roof.' He grinned. 'I knew we'd have some fun here.'

'No.' Lux reached across the table and picked up another satellite view. 'The gap between buildings is too wide – you couldn't jump across.'

'Bet I could if I had Charlie's spring shoes.' Slink took the sheet from Lux and examined it a moment. 'What about this?' he said, pointing.

Jack leant in for a closer look.

He was pointing at a wall that separated the alleyway from the yard and ran between the Hindleton and the neighbouring building.

'What about it?' Lux said.

'I go up here,' Slink traced his finger over the wall, 'and along that wall.' He stopped between the buildings. 'I jump across to the apartment block.' He indicated a drainpipe. 'Up that and along the ledge and – bingo – I disable the cameras so that you can break in through the back door undetected.' Slink tossed the sheet on to the table with a flourish.

Lux stared at him. 'You can do that?'

Slink grinned. 'Of course.'

'That might just work,' Jack said, a flood of renewed hope coursing through him.

'It's doable?' Charlie said.

'Yeah. If Slink can climb up there, we stand a chance.' Jack rose from his chair. 'We leave in thirty minutes.'

Before Jack had time to ask her, Lux was sending a text message to her friend Drake.

Slink slapped his hands together. 'About time we had some fun.'

'Fun always gets us into trouble,' Obi said.

Slink beamed at him. 'Exactly.'

• • •

Half an hour later, a yellow taxi turned into Pell Street.

Lux pointed. 'Here he is.'

In the driver's seat was a boy who looked only a year or so older than Jack and Charlie. He had shoulder-length mousy-brown hair, dark brown eyes and wore a bright orange T-shirt.

Jack frowned. 'That's Drake?'

Lux nodded.

'He doesn't look old enough to drive.'

Lux shrugged. The taxi pulled up in front of them and she opened the passenger door. 'Hey, Drake.'

'Hey.'

Lux gestured at the others as she climbed into the passenger seat. 'This is Jack, Charlie, Slink and Wren.'

'Nice to meet you,' Charlie said.

Drake winked. 'Nice accent.'

Charlie blushed and turned away.

Wren stared at Drake. 'He's pretty,' she whispered.

Slink snorted as he opened the back door. 'Boys can't be pretty.'

Wren glowered at him. 'Why not?'

Slink went to answer, but Charlie said, 'I think he's pretty too, Wren.' Her eyes flitted to Jack and she climbed into the back seat.

Wren stuck her tongue out at Slink and clambered in after her.

Letting out an annoyed breath, Slink got in too.

Jack managed to squeeze in and close the door.

As Drake pulled away, Jack explained what the plan was, and ran it through several times, so that by the time they were driving through Central Park, everyone knew exactly what they had to do.

Jack thought it seemed eerie at night, with its trees casting strange shadows.

Drake stopped the taxi and turned in his seat to face them. 'You want me to wait at the rendezvous point like you said?'

Jack nodded. 'Thanks. We might need to get away fast.'

'Go get this Hector idiot,' Drake said. 'He's hurt a lot of our friends.'

'I know,' Jack said. 'We'll do what we can.'

'What about me?' Lux said. 'What shall I do?'

'Could you wait here and keep an eye out for the police?'

'No problem.'

Jack, Charlie, Slink and Wren pulled up their hoods and bandanas and jumped out.

As he watched Drake drive off towards Fifth Avenue, a strange feeling of foreboding washed over him – he hated not having enough time to plan missions properly.

Mind you, it was as crazy as their usual plans, so it should work.

'Everyone clear on what we have to do?' he said to the others.

The three of them nodded.

Jack pressed a finger to his ear. 'Obi?'

'Commander Obi here.'

Jack looked at Charlie.

She smiled back at him. 'Let it go,' she whispered. 'Where's the harm in it?'

Jack let out a slow breath. 'OK, *Commander.*'

Slink snorted. 'Idiot.'

Jack shot him a look. 'What visuals you got?'

'I have four,' Obi said. 'Two cameras at the front of the buildings, a little way down the road.

One of them is on a motorised mount and I can just make out the roof of the apartment when I tilt it up.'

'Good,' Jack said. 'Any lights on inside?'

'Yep. Both sets of top windows.'

'What else have you got?'

There was a short pause then Obi said, 'I've hacked into another two cameras. One is a block away and I just saw Drake heading to the meeting spot. The last camera is pointing down the alleyway at the back of the buildings. It's dark, but I'll be able to tell if anyone goes there too.'

'Thanks. Keep us updated.' Jack motioned for the others to follow him down a narrow path between the trees.

In the distance, he could make out the shimmer of a lake. The park looked so natural – like it had been here for ever and the modern buildings had just sprung up around it.

They reached Fifth Avenue. Jack stopped and turned around slowly, looking about to make sure they were alone. Satisfied they were, he nodded at Slink and they both knelt down.

By their feet was a large manhole cover, which they prised open with crowbars.

Jack pulled a torch from his pocket and shone it down the hole. A metal ladder disappeared below. He stood up and glanced at Wren. 'Will you be OK on your own?'

She stared down and swallowed. 'Yeah.'

'There'll be rats,' Slink said. 'American rats are vicious little bug–'

'*Slink.*' Charlie squeezed Wren's arm. 'You'll be fine.'

Wren glanced uneasily at her. 'I know.' Though she didn't sound convinced.

Charlie checked Wren's backpack was zipped up and secure. 'She's good to go.'

Jack handed Wren a torch and she flicked it on, sat down and swung her legs into the hole. With another furtive glance up at the others, she dropped inside and descended the ladder.

Jack watched as Wren reached the bottom, shone the beam of her torch left and right, then disappeared.

He slid the manhole cover back into position and straightened up. 'Let's go.'

Gathering up the crowbars, they hopped over the wall, jogged across the road and circled the buildings, heading down the alleyway that ran along the back of them.

Charlie shone her torch on the ground ahead. After a moment she stopped. 'Here it is,' she whispered. By her feet was another manhole cover.

Jack and Slink knelt down, jammed their crowbars into the edge and loosened it.

Finally Jack straightened up. 'Remember,' he said to Charlie, 'once you've helped us' – he handed her a crowbar – 'come back here and open it as planned.'

Charlie nodded and slipped the crowbar into her backpack.

The three of them continued up the alley until they reached a gate that led to the yard at the back of the apartment building.

Jack held up his hand, stopping Charlie and Slink in their tracks. He pointed upwards. There was a camera covering the back door, the yard and its gate.

Charlie shrugged off her backpack, unzipped it and pulled out a pair of wire cutters. She handed them to Slink. 'Remember to stay out of view of the cameras.'

'Yeah, yeah, I've got this.' Slink slipped the cutters into his pocket and looked up at the wall.

It was at least four metres tall, and narrow.

'You sure you can make that?' Jack said to him.

'Easy...Obi, hit it.'

Dubstep blared through their headsets and Slink bounced lightly on the balls of his feet, psyching himself up as the music built in intensity. He hunched down. 'Here it comes.'

The track erupted into an enormous cacophony of bass that vibrated the inside of Jack's skull.

Slink leapt forward and ran directly at the corner where the back wall met the wall that divided the buildings, then sprang his right foot on to the wall to his right, then his left on the left-hand wall and repeated this until he was on the top.

Jack's jaw dropped.

Slink smiled down at them both. 'See?' he whispered into his headset.

That had been, without doubt, one of the most impressive things Jack had seen Slink do. He shook himself. 'Go.'

With his arms outstretched for balance, the boy hurried along the top of the wall until he was adjacent to the apartment.

He then crouched and sprang at the drainpipe, grabbing it and hauling himself up until he found a ledge above the camera.

He pulled the wire cutters from his pocket and cut the lead at the back of the camera. He then gave them a thumbs-up and made his way down again.

Charlie stepped up to the gate.

It had a padlock and chain. She removed a wallet of lock picks from her jacket pocket and, in less than a minute, the lock clicked.

As quietly as he could, Jack slipped the chain out of the gate and opened it.

After making sure no one was around, he waved Charlie through.

Slink dropped beside them and the three of them hurried across the yard to the back door.

Charlie examined the lock. 'Like I thought,' she whispered. 'This would take too long to pick.' She reached into her bag and pulled out a plastic tube with a plunger on one end and a cup on the other.

'What's that?' Slink said.

'Acid.' Charlie fixed the cup over the lock. 'Stand back. Serene said this stuff is seriously corrosive.' She twisted the end and the plunger started to depress.

The three of them backed away as the lock hissed.

After several seconds, the plunger stopped and there was a cracking sound.

Charlie carefully stepped up to the door and opened it. 'OK, it's safe.' She looked at Jack. 'See you at the rendezvous point, and good luck.'

Luck, Jack thought, was something they definitely would need from here on in.

'Come on,' he whispered to Slink, and they crept into the building.

They were now standing in a hallway. Ahead, at the far end, Jack could see the door that led to the lobby.

To the left of the door were mailboxes built into the wall, with a padded bench under them. To the right was a flight of stairs leading up.

Jack glanced at Slink, put a finger to his lips, and nodded. They moved silently along the hallway.

The only sound came from a TV playing somewhere.

They reached the bottom of the stairs and crept up them.

As they reached the third floor, a noise made them freeze – it was muffled shouting.

Ahead, a door opened and a man appeared. He turned back, shouted several swear words, then slammed the door shut behind him.

Red-faced and sweating, he marched towards Jack and Slink.

They didn't move.

The man snarled at them, 'What are you looking at?'

'Nothing,' Jack said.

The man leant into Jack's face. 'That's what I thought.' His breath stank. He glanced back at the door, then looked at Jack and Slink again. 'Get out of my way.' He shoved past and muttered, 'Damn gutter punk kids.' He almost stumbled down the stairs, then disappeared.

'What's a gutter punk?' Slink whispered into Jack's ear.

Jack shrugged. 'No idea.'

'I like it,' Slink said, as he followed Jack up to the next floor. 'Gutter punk. The Urban Gutter Punks.'

After climbing several more flights of stairs, Jack and Slink pushed open the door to the roof and cool air greeted them.

They looked across Central Park. Now they were up there, Jack was surprised how high it was – the trees looked so small.

He stayed by the door.

Slink glanced at him. 'The height thing again?'

Jack nodded.

Slink smiled. 'With all the stuff you've had to do, I would've thought you'd be way over that by now.'

'Me too.' Jack took a breath and followed Slink across the rooftop.

'There's nothing to worry about.' Slink winked and dropped over the edge of the building.

Jack fell to his knees, his heart hammering so hard it threatened to burst through his chest, and peered down.

Just a couple of metres below was a balcony.

Slink stood on it, looking up and grinning.

'Really *not* funny, Slink,' Jack hissed.

Slink moved to the French windows and peered through a gap in the curtains. After a minute, he crept along the balcony, sprang up on to the handrail and crossed the narrow gap to the next.

Above, Jack mirrored him.

Slink peered through another set of glass doors for a moment, then stepped back. 'OK,' he whispered. 'You were right – it's two balconies per apartment. This one is the bedroom. There's no one in there.'

'What about the other one?' Jack whispered.

'There's an old bloke in a chair, reading a book. Behind him was a old woman sitting at a desk, writing something.'

'OK,' Jack said. 'Move on.'

The gap to the next balcony was at least a couple of metres away. Jack was about to help Slink up to the roof, but he took a few steps back and leapt the gap.

Jack sighed. 'Do you always have to do it the dangerous way?'

Slink shrugged. 'Yeah, mostly.' He peered through the next set of doors, spending a lot longer looking through them than before, shifting his weight from side to side. Without a word, he vaulted across to the last balcony and repeated the process. Finally he pulled back and looked up. 'I think it's empty.'

'Are you sure?' Jack said.

'Pretty sure. The rooms look clean. No glasses or cups on the side. No bags or clothes. The bed's been made.'

Jack hesitated. The first apartment had an old couple in it. The second was empty. Had his hunch been right? Maybe Hector wasn't here at all. But he had to be, Jack knew it.

'Hey,' Slink hissed. 'What do we do?'

'I need to see for myself.' Jack sat on the edge of the roof and looked down. His stomach lurched.

'Want some dubstep?' Slink said.

'Not even a little bit.'

Slink hopped up on to the handrail and guided Jack down.

When he was safe on the balcony, Jack peered through the door to the sitting room. Slink was right – the apartment looked clean and tidy, like no one was there.

Bracing himself, Jack stepped over the railing to the other balcony and peered through that door. It was the same story here – everything in the bedroom looked pristine, as if no one was staying there. Surely even the tidiest people would leave some sign of their presence?

Jack was about to pull back when he noticed something under one of the bedside tables – it was a chewing gum wrapper folded neatly into the shape of a bird. It looked like a crow or a raven of some kind.

A rush of adrenalin coursed through Jack. 'This is it. Hector's been here.' He pressed a finger to his ear and said, 'Wren, you're up.'

CHAPTER
SIX

AT FIRST NOTHING HAPPENED. THEN THERE WAS
a distant popping sound and the lights in the apartment went out.

'Hope she didn't just blow herself up,' Slink said.

'I'm OK,' came a breathless reply. Wren was obviously running.

She'd planted a device that sent a powerful pulse through the apartment's electrical system. It wasn't enough to do any lasting damage, just trip a few switches and temporarily disable the alarm.

Jack and Slink had a few minutes before someone turned the electricity supply back on.

Slink took out a set of lock picks and quickly opened the doors from the balcony. Once inside, they stood there for a moment, surveying their surroundings.

'What are we looking for?' Slink asked.

'Clues.'

Jack's eyes moved from one object to the next: the bed, wardrobe, bathroom door, carpet...They finally rested on the origami chewing gum wrapper under the bedside table. It was the only sign that Hector had been in the room.

'Can you check the bathroom?' Jack tiptoed over to the bedside table and silently opened the drawers.

Both were empty.

He shut the drawers and stepped over to the wardrobe. It was empty too, apart from a few coat hangers.

'Nothing in here,' Slink said, coming back from the bathroom.

Jack hurried to the sitting room.

It was spacious with a crystal chandelier, hand-carved furniture and real oil paintings on the walls.

The apartment reminded him of Hector's hotel suite in London – the one where Hector and the fake agents that worked for him had held Jack hostage.

It was tidy, with no sign anyone had been there recently. Jack walked across to a desk on the far wall and opened the drawer, but it was empty too.

'So,' Slink said, 'what's the verdict?'

'Hector's been here, but they were careful to clean up. I have no idea if they left ten minutes ago or last week.'

'You think that receptionist tipped them off about you?'

'I'm not sure.'

'Guys?' Charlie said in their ears. 'Are you OK?'

'We're fine,' Slink said.

Jack noticed a utility cupboard by the door and opened it.

The top shelf was empty and there was a pile of towels at the bottom.

Jack lifted the towels aside. 'What's all this?'

Underneath were several batteries, reels of wire, a bag of computer components, a police radio and a large homemade circuit board.

'Can you hold that up?' Jack said.

Slink picked up the circuit board and Jack took several pictures with one of Serene's phones Charlie had given him. 'OK. Put it back as it was.'

They heard voices coming from the hallway.

Jack took the circuit board from Slink, returned it to the bottom of the cupboard and covered it with the towels again.

As he closed the door, the voices grew louder.

Jack and Slink hurried through the bedroom and back out on to the balcony.

'Get us out of here,' Jack whispered.

Slink nodded and climbed up the front of the building.

Suddenly the lights inside the apartment came on.

Jack clambered over the railing to the apartment's other balcony. He slipped off his backpack, pulled out a camera with a suction cup attached and stuck it to the glass, right in the corner of the doors, facing into the room.

'Obi?' he whispered.

'Yeah?'

'Have you got the feed from this camera?'

'Hold on.'

A rope dropped in front of Jack's face. He grabbed the end and tied it to his harness.

'Yeah, I've got it,' Obi said. 'Coming through clean.'

'Hey,' Slink hissed.

Jack held up a hand. 'Obi, can you see the front door?'

'Yes.'

'OK.' Jack gave a thumbs-up and Slink supported him as he climbed clumsily on to the roof, careful not to look down.

They jogged to the other side, where Slink looped the climbing rope around an air vent and checked it would hold their weight.

When he was done, he turned to Jack. 'You wanna go first?'

Jack shook his head.

Slink smiled, stood on the lip of the roof, then dropped backwards and started to abseil down the rear of the building.

As Jack watched Slink descend, he wondered if Hector was miles away or whether he'd seen any of this – if he had, the entire mission would've been for nothing.

• • •

Back at Serene's loft, Slink told Lux, Drake and the others what they'd found in the apartment.

Wren looked thoughtful. 'So you think Hector will come back for that circuit board and radio?'

Jack shrugged. 'Probably not him, but someone might.'

At least he hoped so.

'Monday,' Slink said, obviously remembering Hector's giant henchman. 'I bet he goes back for it.'

'Or Connor and Cloud,' Wren said with obvious disgust. 'They'll be with Hector too.'

The Outlaws had been chased by Connor many times before. Jack could picture his snarling, twisted face all too easily.

Charlie stood and held out her hand. 'Can I have a peek at those pictures of the circuit board you took?'

Jack passed her the phone.

Charlie scrolled through the pictures and frowned at them for a long while, turning the phone left and right and muttering under her breath. Finally she handed the phone back to him.

'What is it then?' he said.

'I'm not completely sure,' Charlie said, 'but if I was to bet on it – I reckon it's a circuit they've made to extract, decode and decompile the virus.'

Drake crossed his arms. 'Come again?'

'It's a custom piece of hardware they used to take apart the virus's program.'

Jack sighed. 'God knows what Hector's up to now. But I'm sure that he won't want anyone getting their hands on it.'

Charlie pointed at the screen in Serene's office – it displayed the CCTV image of the apartment. 'As soon as someone goes back there, Jack, we've got them. It's not over yet.'

'I've set the computer to let off an alarm as soon as it detects any movement,' Obi said.

Jack nodded. 'Good thinking.'

'Well,' Drake said, yawning and standing up, 'I need some sleep.' He moved towards the spiral staircase. 'Let me know when you need me again.'

'Thanks for helping us,' Jack said.

'No problem.' He waved and disappeared.

Now it was Lux who was yawning. 'You mind if I crash here the night?'

'No,' Obi said, a little too quickly.

Lux smiled. 'I'll use Serene's room. Night.' She strode through the office and into Serene's bedroom, closing the door behind her.

'I think it's time we got some sleep too,' Charlie said.

Charlie, Obi and Wren got busy unrolling beds and sleeping bags while Slink called to check on his mum again.

Jack didn't move. He just stared at the screen in the office. He felt so helpless – catching up with Hector all rested on someone going back to the apartment to retrieve the parts they'd left behind.

'Awesome,' he muttered.

• • •

The next day passed painfully slowly. And the next. By the third day, Jack had practically given up all hope of finding Hector.

Every news channel was filled with stories about hackers attacking New York and it was getting worse – spreading out from the city. It seemed as if there was another police raid and an arrest every hour. The reporters thought it was some kind of coordinated attack, by tens, if not hundreds, of hackers.

Truth was, it was all one kid: Quentin Del Sarto – aka Hector – and his new hacking tool, causing disruption wherever he went. By the time afternoon had come on the third day, Jack and the others were going stir crazy. Everyone was snapping at each other and bickering over petty things, like whether to watch cartoons or conspiracy theories.

When Slink hit Obi over the back of the head with the remote control, Jack stepped in. 'OK,' he said, snatching it from him and switching off the TV. 'I think it's time we planned some extra missions.'

'What missions?' Obi said.

'RAKing.'

This got everyone's attention.

'When you say RAKing,' Lux said. 'Do you mean Random Acts of Kindness?'

'You know what it is?' Obi said.

Lux nodded. 'Of course.'

'It's the best thing ever,' Wren said.

Jack glanced out of the window. 'Only problem is, we need to come up with some ideas.'

Lux smiled. 'I have a few thoughts.'

Slink and Wren jumped to their feet, and for the first time in days, they looked excited.

'I need time to prepare.' Lux hurried over to the spiral staircase. She stopped and turned back to Charlie. 'Everyone is going to need a cell phone.'

'I can cover that,' Charlie said. 'Serene has plenty.'

'Good. I'll call Drake and ask him to come get you.'

'Where are we going?' Wren said.

'You'll see.' Lux disappeared down the stairs.

• • •

An hour later, Jack, Charlie, Slink, Wren, Obi and Drake were standing on a balcony overlooking the main concourse in Grand Central Station.

The interior of the building was gigantic – with massive square columns, tall arched windows and a polished marble floor. It even had a green ceiling with star constellations.

Wren stared up at it, open-mouthed. 'This place is amazing.'

'I know.' Slink looked like he was itching to climb up there.

Lux appeared from the crowd and jogged up the stairs. She reached into her backpack and handed Obi a stack of yellow cards in clear plastic envelopes. 'Hold these a minute, please.'

Obi turned them over. On the back of each one was a strip of double-sided tape.

'What are these?' he said.

'Prepaid Metrocards.'

'Like the Underground?' Wren said.

'Exactly like that, yeah.'

'What are we doing with them?' Slink asked.

'Geocaching, or my version of it anyway.'

Wren blinked. 'Huh?'

Lux took her mobile phone from her pocket. 'I do this every few months. Makes me happy again if I've been having a tough time.' She looked between them all. 'Everyone got their phones?'

They nodded and held them up.

'Great,' Lux said. 'Open the map application. In the top corner you'll see GPS coordinates.'

They all did as she asked.

'OK!' Jack said, catching on to what Lux had in mind. 'Can I have a couple of those envelopes?' he asked Obi.

Obi handed him two.

Charlie frowned at Jack. 'You know what this is about?'

'Yep.' Jack gestured around the station. 'Go hide them. Each time you do, make a note of the GPS co-ordinates on the phone.'

Charlie stared a moment, then her eyes widened. 'Oh, I get it.'

'I don't,' Wren said. 'What's going on?'

Lux winked. 'You'll see.'

Everyone hurried off in different directions.

Jack strode over to the information desk. He glanced around to make sure no one was watching him, then stuck the envelope to the underside of the counter.

He copied the GPS coordinates to a note file and headed towards the stairs at the far end of the station.

Jack leant against them a moment and tried to look casual as he stuck a second envelope to the side of the stone steps.

After making sure it was secure, and taking a note of the coordinates again, he hurried up the stairs and stood on the balcony, overlooking the entire station.

Lux joined him. 'You didn't hide them *too* well, did you?' she asked.

'I don't think so.'

A few minutes later, everyone was standing on the balcony.

Lux took each of their phones and copied the different sets of GPS coordinates to her own.

'Now what?' Obi asked her.

'Now we wait.'

As they stood there, for the first time in a long while, Jack felt at peace. The sun cut through the windows, bathing the interior in an orange hue. People hurried to catch trains, while others waited to be reunited with loved ones. All the while, Jack and the others watched from above.

Detached.

Tranquil.

'Look.' Wren pointed at the information desk where Jack had hidden the first of his envelopes.

A girl in her early twenties had her phone held in front of her and was studying the screen. She glanced around, then ran her hand under the edge of the information desk.

'Warm...' Jack muttered.

She stepped to her left.

'Warmer...'

Another step.

'Hot.'

The girl pulled out the envelope.

'Bingo.'

She opened it and took out the Metrocard. Her eyes almost popped from their sockets. She stood there a moment, then, beaming from ear to ear, hurried off towards the subway.

Wren looked at Lux. 'How did she know?'

Lux held up her own phone. 'I wrote this application last year. It's called GeoGiftCards or GGC for short. GGC sends the envelope's GPS coordinates as a text to a random person in the area.'

'One each,' Drake added.

'Yeah,' Lux said. 'One set of coordinates each.' She gestured to the other side of the station as a man with long blonde hair walked over to a bin, checking his phone.

'That's my one,' Wren said, her eyes lighting up.

The man leant over the bin and removed the envelope. He slid out the card, smiled to himself, then glanced around before disappearing into the crowd of commuters.

For the next half an hour, more people came and went, each finding their prize and hurrying off with a satisfied look on their face.

When the last envelope was found, Lux slipped her phone back into her pocket. 'What do you think?'

'We'll have to steal that idea,' Charlie said.

'You're welcome to.'

Jack agreed – he thought it was a fantastic thing to do and was thinking of other things, besides Metro cards, they could hide. They would try it out in London as soon as they had the chance. The number of places to stash envelopes was mind-boggling – literally millions – and he couldn't wait to give it a go.

'It's awesome,' Wren said as they walked back to the entrance. 'What other ideas do you have?'

'I have one,' Drake said. 'If no one minds?'

'Go for it,' Jack said. If it was anything like Lux's gifting app, this should be a lot of fun.

· · ·

Drake 'acquired' a new car – this one was a dark blue sedan – and drove them to a place called Jersey City, across the Hudson River.

It was similar to New York, with tall buildings at its centre, only they were fewer and spaced further apart.

Drake stopped at a graveyard at the edge of the city and looked at the clock on the dashboard. 'Perfect timing.'

'For what?' Wren said, peering out of the window.

Drake pointed at a man crossing the road in front of them. 'Him.'

The man wore an old brown suit with frayed cuffs. He also wore a Fedora and scuffed black shoes.

'Who's he?' Obi said.

They all continued to watch as the man limped through the entrance of the graveyard and up the path.

'His name is Mr Percival,' Drake said. 'He comes here at this time every day. Every day for at least the last seventeen years.'

'Seventeen years?' Charlie said.

'I grew up just there.' Drake pointed down the road to a line of houses. 'I've know Mr Percival all my life. He lives off a small war pension. He can't afford much.'

'What can we do for him?' Jack said.

'I've tried giving him money; he won't accept it.' Drake reached down by the seat and pulled out a bunch of flowers. 'I bought these earlier. They're for his wife's grave.' Drake handed them to Charlie. 'Will you do it?'

She stared at him a moment. 'You want me to –'

'Yeah.' Drake nodded at Mr Percival as he continued up the path.

Charlie took a breath, then opened the door and climbed out.

Mr Percival stopped at a grave marked with a headstone in the shape of a cross, removed his hat and bowed his head.

Charlie walked over to him, said something and handed Mr Percival the flowers.

He hesitated, then took them from her, and Charlie spent a few minutes talking to him before finally returning to the car.

As they drove away, Wren said, 'What did you say to him?'

Charlie glanced at her. 'I asked him to take the flowers. Then I told him that there were people who'd always care about him and his wife.'

• • •

Back at Serene's loft, Obi had a message for Jack.

It was from the Shepherd.

Jack scanned the email and his chest tightened as he read what mission the Shepherd wanted them to do.

Finally he straightened up, hardly believing what he'd just read.

'How are we going to do that?' Obi said. 'It's impossible.'

Jack closed his eyes and pinched the bridge of his nose. 'I have no idea.'

Just when he'd thought things couldn't get any worse.

CHAPTER SEVEN

JACK WALKED OVER TO CHARLIE, SLINK, WREN and Lux in the lounge area. 'There's another mission we've got to do. It's for the Shepherd.' He hesitated. 'And I need everyone's help with it.'

Truth was, he needed a miracle.

'What is it?' Charlie said, noticing his glum expression.

'The "what" isn't a problem so much,' Jack said. 'It's the "where" that's an issue.'

They all looked puzzled by this.

'OK,' Slink said. 'So *where* is it?'

'Los Angeles.'

Slink laughed. 'Right.'

Obi joined the group and sat on one of the sofas.

'No,' Jack said. 'I'm serious.'

'This is the east coast, Jack,' Lux said, incredulous. 'LA is on the west coast.'

'In case you haven't noticed,' Slink added, 'this country is quite big.'

'I know, but we don't have a choice. If we can't do this mission somehow, we won't be able to go home.'

This was greeted with stunned silence.

Slink stood up. 'Say that again.'

Jack then proceeded to tell them all about the deal he'd made with the Shepherd. 'We do this mission and he'll let us fly home.'

'Wait a minute.' Slink's face reddened. 'You couldn't have told us this *before* we left England?'

'I didn't think it would be a problem,' Jack said. 'I thought he'd want us to do something in New York. Something small. I wasn't expecting –'

'Oh, right.' Slink glared at him. 'Well, that's OK then.' His face twisted into anger. 'Why didn't you check with him first, Jack? You know I can't risk getting stuck here. You know my mum –'

Jack held up his hands. 'I'm really, really sorry, Slink. I didn't know this would happen. We won't get stuck here. We'll find a way to do the mission and get home. All right?'

'No, Jack,' Slink snapped. 'Really *not* all right. Like, it's so far from all right, you can hardly see it.

The "all right" is a freakin speck in the distance.' He stormed off, slamming into Jack's shoulder as he went. *Idiot.*

'Slink,' Charlie called after him. 'Please.'

Slink spun back. 'What? You're gonna side with him, I suppose?' He waved a finger at her. 'You promised me too, Charlie. Remember?'

'I know, Slink, I –' She looked at Jack. 'What do we do?'

Jack shook his head and stared up at the ceiling.

The fact of the matter was, Slink was right. If Jack had known what the Shepherd had planned, he wouldn't have asked Slink to risk it by coming with them. They would've had to manage without him somehow.

Jack squeezed his eyes closed.

The Shepherd had really done them over with this one.

The room was uncomfortably silent for a long while.

Jack glanced at Slink skulking in the corner, but he wouldn't make eye contact. He was leaning against a pillar, arms crossed, scowling at the floor.

Lux stood up. 'Let me see if I can get some help.' She hurried off to Serene's office.

'What does the Shepherd want us to do?' Wren said in a small voice, as though she was worried she'd set Slink off shouting again.

Jack looked at her. 'According to his email, we have to go to an address near Hollywood and steal a laptop. He's sent a map like the one of RAF Hillgate, but that's it. No further instructions.'

'It's OK,' Lux said, returning to the group. 'Drake is sorting it out. He can get us there.'

Jack blinked. 'What? How?'

'He's got a friend who's a pilot. He's good. *Very* good. Works for a private charter company.'

Jack stared at her. 'How old is this guy?' He had visions of a sixteen-year-old wrestling with aeroplane controls while they plummeted to the earth at five hundred miles an hour. But he also had to admit he felt a huge amount of relief that someone might be able to help them, and he was grateful to Lux and Drake. 'Thank you. I don't know how –'

'It's fine,' Lux said.

Jack looked over at Slink and noticed his frown had softened slightly.

Thank goodness, Jack thought. Because they were going to need him.

'I'm calling Mum,' Slink muttered, heading off to Serene's office.

'Right,' Jack said to Lux. 'I could really do with your help planning this mission. You in?'

• • •

Three hours later, Jack, Charlie, Slink, Wren and Lux were on the tarmac at MacArthur Airport on Long Island, just east of New York City.

Obi had stayed back at the loft, keeping an eye out for Hector or for any movement at the Hindleton Building.

The Outlaws expected to be gone less than twenty-four hours, but Obi had plenty of food supplies to keep him going.

'Hey.' Drake strode over to them and winked at Charlie and Wren. 'How you doing?'

They both beamed at him.

Everyone shielded their eyes and squinted as a blue jumbo jet came in to land.

'Is that it?' Slink asked Drake, looking hopeful.

'No.' Drake pointed. '*This* is our ride.'

A sleek private jet emerged from a hangar and taxied over to them.

'We're going on that?' Wren said, open-mouthed.

Drake nodded. 'Yeah. Pretty cool, huh?'

The jet stopped in front of them, and after a moment, the door opened and a set of steps unfurled.

A man in a pilot's uniform hurried down and came over to them. He nodded at Drake. 'Howdy.'

They shook hands.

'Jon.' Drake stepped back and gestured at the others. 'These are friends of mine from England.'

There was a flicker of confusion as Jon's eyes moved over the Outlaws, but he quickly recovered. 'Of course,' he said. 'Good to meet you all.' He motioned to the jet. 'Shall we?'

Inside, five pairs of comfortable swivel chairs sat facing each other, each with small round tables between them.

Jack didn't want to think about how much it must be costing someone to get them to the other side of the country. It was money they could've spent on RAKing.

Slink dropped his backpack to the floor, leapt into one of the seats and spun it around in circles. 'This is freakin awesome. Beats some stupid crate where we have to stand still for, like, eight hours.'

The others slipped off their backpacks and sat down too.

'I've arranged for us to land at an airport outside Los Angeles,' Jon said to Drake. 'It's a little way out, but I've taken care of security. You shouldn't have any problems.'

Drake smiled. 'Thanks.'

Jon walked to the cockpit door. 'Oh,' he turned back, 'and I've organised a rental car for you. Gave them false details, so you can use that other licence you've got.' He glanced at the Outlaws, then said in a hushed voice in Drake's ear, 'I didn't want you to have to "find" a car when you got there.' He cleared his throat and disappeared into the cockpit.

'What's the deal with him?' Slink asked Drake.

Drake sat down. 'What do you mean?'

Slink snorted and gestured around. 'This must be costing a fortune. How come he's doing it?'

That was exactly what Jack wanted to know.

'I saved his wife from a fire,' Drake said.

They all stared at him.

After a moment's stunned silence, Charlie said, 'Really?'

'Yeah. Really.'

'I was there too,' Lux said, 'but I only caught the end of what happened.'

The engines started up and the plane moved towards the runway.

Wren leant forward in her seat and rested her chin on her hands. 'Tell us what happened.'

Drake kept his voice low. 'Well, Lux and me were working on a job. Some dude had stolen data from a friend of ours.' He glanced out of the window and back again. 'He lived in Queens, another borough located to the east of Manhattan.'

'We passed a sign for it on the way,' Charlie said.

'Yeah, I was supposed to be meeting Drake there, but I got delayed,' Lux said. 'We were running out of time, so –'

'I had to break into the guy's house myself,' Drake continued. 'It was easy – I recovered the data and destroyed his hard drives. I was just leaving when I noticed smoke coming from the place next door. It was pouring from the roof. I went to head off, but my conscience got the better of me and I turned back.' He glanced between them. 'There could have been kids in there.'

'You went in?' Wren said, her eyes wide.

'Yeah.'

'There's no way I would've gone back,' Charlie said.

No surprises there, Jack thought. Charlie's biggest fear was being trapped in a fire.

'What happened then?' Wren's voice was barely above a whisper.

'Well,' Drake said, 'I went upstairs. When I opened the bedroom door, a wall of heat hit me.' Drake rolled up his sleeves and revealed burn scars covering his lower arms.

Wren gasped.

Drake tugged at his sleeves, covering his arms again. He glanced at the cockpit door. 'No kids, but I pulled a woman from the fire and somehow I managed to carry her out into the street.'

Adrenalin, Jack thought. He'd been in dangerous situations and had found extra strength.

'You were very brave,' Charlie said.

Drake waved her comment off like a fly. 'I had to go in. I'd never have forgiven myself if I didn't. I feel a bit bad though.'

'For what?' Slink said.

He laughed. 'This is the first time I've asked him for a favour.'

'Well,' Jack said, 'we can't thank you enough. Now we owe you big time.' He glanced at Slink.

The plane turned and stopped.

'Safety belts,' Lux said.

They fastened their belts and the jet powered up the runway and into the sky.

• • •

It took five and a half hours to reach their destination in California. True to Jon's word, an SUV was waiting in the airport car park.

Drake then drove them into Los Angeles.

As they drew near to the main city, Slink sang, 'We're the kids in America, whoa-oh,' for the millionth time.

'Slink!' Charlie snapped.

'Yeah?'

'Can you not?'

'What is that song?' Wren said.

Slink grinned. 'A classic.'

Wren frowned. 'I've never heard it before.'

'I hope we never do again,' Jack muttered. He had to admit, Slink was getting on his nerves too, especially as he couldn't even sing in tune. Though, thinking about it, it did beat Slink's usual choice of blasting everyone's ears with dubstep. And, Jack had to admit, he still felt guilty about risking their return journey to England.

Slink opened his mouth to start singing again, but Charlie shot him a look. 'You sing that one more time and I'll actually throw you out of the car.'

Jack glanced at Lux. She seemed to be having trouble suppressing a laugh.

Wren pressed her face against the glass as they drove past the Hollywood sign that was perched high in the hills to their right. 'Amazing.'

'It looks fake,' Slink said, seeming unimpressed. 'Like a toy town.'

Lux glanced at him. 'Tinseltown,' she said. 'And it's a whole other world out there.'

What time is it in London? Jack thought. *Or in New York, for that matter?*

Travelling across time zones was a weird feeling – especially as they were still in the same country. Though, looking out of the window, Jack found that hard to believe. Lux was right – it was like another world.

They were now driving down a busy street packed with shops and tourists.

'I thought I'd come this way for you guys,' Drake said.

'Hollywood Boulevard,' Lux said, answering the Outlaws' puzzled expressions. 'They call it the Walk of Fame.' She pointed at a Chinese theatre. 'This is where all the famous actors and actresses have their stars put into the sidewalk.'

'Can we stop?' Wren said, almost breathless with excitement. She turned to Jack. 'Please?'

'Can we can spare a few minutes?' he asked Lux.

She nodded.

Wren squealed.

Drake pulled to the kerb behind a tour bus and the others hopped out.

'Be quick,' he said. 'There's no parking.'

Wren and Slink hurried through the crowd of tourists and when Jack, Charlie and Lux caught up with them, Wren was lying on the ground with her arms stretched out.

Charlie laughed. 'What are you doing?'

'Marilyn Monroe.' Wren had her hands pressed into the concrete where the movie star had made an impression.

Above the handprints was Marilyn Monroe's signature, drawn into the concrete. In the corner were the numbers 6.26.53.

Wren looked up. 'She's the same lady from Badbury platform, right, Jack?'

He nodded, remembering the old poster – it was for a film called *Some Like It Hot*.

After a minute, Wren clambered to her feet and rushed around the other handprints.

Most were from way before any of them were born, but there were some Jack recognised, like Arnold Schwarzenegger, Jim Carrey, Bruce Willis and Tom Cruise.

• • •

Ten minutes later, Jack, Charlie, Slink, Wren and Lux were back in the car and Drake was driving up a hill just off Hollywood Boulevard.

The road was winding and narrow and, as they climbed, the houses got bigger, as if they were expanding in the thinning atmosphere.

'Where are we going?' Charlie asked.

'Burbank.' Drake checked the GPS. 'We've got to go through the Hollywood hills to get there.'

• • •

Finally they came to a giant studio building.

'OK,' Jack said, turning to the others. 'Lux and I looked at this place and there's no way in without getting caught.'

Slink glanced up at the building. 'Bet I could climb it.'

'Not without being seen,' Jack said. 'We've got to do this stealth.'

Slink frowned at him. 'I'm the king of stealth.'

Charlie laughed. 'Yeah, not so much.'

Slink crossed his arms.

'So we're looking for a laptop?' Wren asked Jack.

'Yeah. The Shepherd wants us to go in, find it and take it back home with us.'

'Their security is tight,' Lux said. 'Guards and security barriers on every entrance. So...we're going on a studio tour.'

Wren's mouth fell open. 'We are?'

'Yep,' Jack said.

Wren bounced in her seat. 'Yes, yes, yes!'

They all laughed.

All except Slink – he frowned and looked sullen.

'I got us all tickets online,' Lux said.

Wren grinned. 'This is awesome.'

'It's going to be risky too,' Jack said. 'We need to get it right.' He quickly explained the plan that he and Lux had come up with, then looked at Drake. 'Do you mind waiting for us?'

'No problem,' Drake said. 'I'll park down the street and keep the motor running.'

'Thank you.' Jack opened the door. 'Come on, guys. And remember – no bags.' As he climbed out, the heat of the day hit him like a blast furnace.

Wren sprang from the car and Jack, Charlie and Slink followed her up the path and around the corner.

They entered through a set of sliding glass doors and a security guard waved them through a metal detector.

Wren beamed as Lux got their tickets and they stood in line outside a set of double doors.

'Try to look like tourists,' Jack whispered.

'I don't think that's going to be a problem,' Charlie said, nodding at Wren.

She was now bouncing from foot to foot.

After a few minutes, the door opened and a tour guide led the group outside to a waiting tram.

The Outlaws and Lux climbed into the back.

The tour guide drove into the main studio lot, narrating as he went, and stopped outside a large door. Everyone climbed out and followed the guide on foot into a hangar.

Inside were twenty or so cars and motorcycles, from sports models to superbikes. The tour guide explained what film each one had been in.

Jack and the others stayed at the back of the group.

Jack nudged Charlie's arm and nodded at a side door. She nodded back.

Jack stepped over to Wren. 'Now keep the guide busy, yeah?'

'OK.' She hurried over to the man, who was taking pictures of a couple of members of the group stood in front of a green screen. On the monitor was a picture of a red steam train at a platform with a glass roof.

Once Jack was sure Wren was keeping the tour guide distracted, asking him a million questions, he stepped over to the side door with the others.

Charlie pulled a purse from her pocket and peeled part of the seam back, revealing a secret compartment with several ceramic lock picks. She slid two out, quickly unlocked the door and straightened up. 'OK.'

'See you in the museum part of the tour in half an hour,' Jack whispered.

He backed through the door with Slink and Lux and closed it behind them.

Hopefully, if all went to plan, Wren and Charlie would keep the tour guide busy enough not to realise he'd just lost three young members of his group.

Jack, Slink and Lux jogged down a corridor, opened a door at the end and stepped outside.

There was another giant warehouse in front of them.

Lux looked at her phone, consulting the map from the Shepherd, then pointed. 'That way.'

Jack hurried to the corner of the warehouse and peered around it.

There was a short road that ended with a fence. On each side of the road were the backs of buildings with their fire escapes. To his right was a plastic skip on wheels.

'No one's here,' Jack whispered. He checked for cameras, then motioned for the others to follow him.

Keeping close to the wall of the left-hand ware-house, they jogged along until they reached a side door.

Jack glanced about, double-checking they weren't being watched, then tried the handle, but it was locked. 'What?' He glanced at Lux.

She examined the map and shrugged. 'It says to go through there. Should be unlocked.'

'Great.' Jack looked up at the fire escape. Several storeys above them was another door.

Perhaps they could get in that way.

Jack turned to Slink. 'Can you get the ladder down?'

'Yeah. Help me with this.'

They ran over to the skip and wheeled it under the fire escape. Slink then leapt on top, and as he pulled the ladder down, it let out a deafening squeak.

Slink winced, paused for a moment, then yanked the ladder down the rest of the way in one swift movement. It let out another squeak – higher-pitched this time – and clattered to a stop on the concrete below. He jumped on to the ladder and raced up the fire escape.

Jack grabbed one of the lower rungs. 'Keep an eye out,' he whispered to Lux. 'We'll check it out.'

She nodded.

Jack climbed the ladder after Slink and reached the first landing of the fire escape.

He looked down and even though he can't have been more than three or four metres above the ground, his stomach lurched and he grabbed the railing for support.

'Hurry up,' Slink hissed down to him. 'We ain't got all day.'

Jack took a deep breath, edged along the landing –
with his back as close to the wall as possible – and
made it to the next metal ladder.

He climbed up to the second landing, repeated
the process and continued up. All the while his
stomach clenched tighter and tighter.

On the third landing, Jack edged his way over to
Slink.

Slink smirked. 'Having fun?'

'No.'

'Good.'

Jack called down to Lux in a low voice: 'You sure
this is the right way?'

She consulted her phone. 'Positive.'

They looked at the door – it was riveted shut with
a metal plate. Jack examined the edges, but it was
no use. If they had a crowbar, they might've been
able to force it open, but without one –

'What about that?' Slink whispered.

A couple of metres along the wall from the fire
escape was a small window. They tried to peer
through it, but they were too far away – the warehouse appeared to be dark inside.

Jack sighed. The climb up there had been a waste
of time.

'I think I can make it,' Slink said.

Jack glanced at him. 'Make what?'

Slink pointed at the window. 'That. Then I can climb down and open the door from the inside.'

The window was a long way from the fire escape and at least ten metres to the ground.

Jack shook his head. 'Too dangerous.'

Slink snorted, and before Jack could stop him, he'd climbed up on to the railing and leapt for the window.

For a split second Jack thought Slink was going to miss, but somehow he managed to grip the bottom of the window frame with just his fingertips.

He looked over at Jack and grinned. Then he hauled himself up and peered through the glass. 'Still can't see anyone. Looks clear.' He shifted his weight, let go with one hand and tried tugging the window frame with the other. 'It's loose.' He braced his feet against the wall, leant back and yanked.

Jack wanted to close his eyes, to order Slink back on to the fire escape, but he knew it was useless. Besides, there was no way Slink could jump back to safety now, it was too far and his feet had nothing but brickwork to support his weight.

Slink pulled a few more times, there was a cracking sound and the window finally hinged up.

He glanced at Jack, then hauled himself through.

After Slink's feet had disappeared, Jack remained motionless, listening, but all he could hear was the blood pounding in his ears.

No alarms.

No shouting.

Not yet anyway.

Jack shook himself, loosened his grip on the railing and edged back along the fire escape.

It took him several nervous minutes to climb down.

Once he was back on the ground, Jack jogged back over to Lux.

A few minutes went by and the lock finally clicked and the door swung open.

'Thank God, Slink.' Jack stepped inside and squinted in the darkness.

There was no one there.

Suddenly a figure dropped in front of him and shouted, 'Arr, harr!'

Jack scrambled backwards, almost tripping over his own feet.

Slink laughed. He was wearing a huge pirate's hat and a waistcoat and was waving a plastic sword in front of him. 'Stay back, ye scurvy dog.'

'What are you doing?' Jack hissed, looking around.

'Relax,' Slink said, sliding the sword into a large belt. 'No one's here. The place is empty.'

Jack took deep breaths, composing himself, trying to slow his heart rate back to a sensible speed. As his eyes adjusted to the gloomy interior, he could see they were standing in a vast warehouse filled with piles of boxes and row upon row of clothes racks.

'Where did you get that outfit?' Lux said to Slink, looking more amused than Jack felt.

'From over there.' Slink gestured past a stack of boxes. 'It was on top of a crate.'

'Props storage,' Lux said.

'Come on,' Jack said, setting off down the gap between the racks.

As they passed hundreds of costumes, Jack caught glimpses of Egyptian dresses, old-fashioned suits, superhero outfits, complete with capes and masks, and a huge variety of hats and shoes. There was even an astronaut's space suit with helmet and backpack.

Slink reached inside a large bin and pulled out two grey sheets of plastic, each in the shape of a person. He waved their arms about and started laughing.

'Inflatable extras. They're used in movies,' Lux said.

Slink's eyebrows rose. 'For what?'

'They put clothes on them and use them in crowd scenes. Saves paying salaries.'

Slink continued to chuckle as he made the plastic people wave at Jack.

'Come on,' Jack said, striding towards the back of the warehouse.

At the end of another row of costumes, they finally found a door.

Lux consulted the map. 'This should be it.'

Jack took a breath, opened the door a few centimetres and peered out into the sunshine.

He blinked at the new scene before him.

It was an old wooden house, painted dark colours. It reminded Jack of the house where Benito Del Sarto had hidden Proteus. In front of the house was a film crew, and a director sat in a chair talking to a woman with headphones and a clipboard.

Several actors dressed as vampires were standing waiting next to a hearse.

To the right of the film set was a row of five trailers.

Lux consulted her phone again and pointed. 'Second one from the front.'

'On it.'

Before Jack could stop him, Slink darted across the road and hid behind the first trailer.

A man carrying a huge light walked past, but he didn't spot Slink.

'Careful,' Jack muttered.

When the guy was gone, Slink hurried to the second trailer. He reached up, gripped the window and lifted himself high enough to peer inside.

Jack held his breath.

A minute later, Slink lowered himself to the ground and darted back over to them.

'Well?' Jack whispered. 'Could you see a laptop?'

'Nah,' Slink said. 'But I could make out the corner of a table and there was a bloke sitting at it. Grey-haired. I bet he's got it.'

'What else?' Jack said.

'Couldn't see anyone else in there. I think the guy's alone, and the other trailers are empty.'

Jack nodded, thinking. He looked at the window at the end of the trailer. 'You think you can open that without him hearing?'

'Yeah. Need a piece of flat metal.' Slink pointed at an air vent sticking out from on top of the trailer. 'Also need to tie a rope to that.'

'I'll get them.' Lux darted off between the racks of costumes.

Jack returned his attention to the trailer. 'Did you see any cameras?'

Slink grinned. 'Of course – four massive ones.'

'Not the studio ones,' Jack said, rolling his eyes. 'I mean did you see any security cameras?'

'Nope.'

'Good.'

Lux came back with a coil of rope and a short sword. She handed them to Slink.

'We move as we originally planned,' Jack said to Lux. 'You're the *lookout*, I'm the *distraction*, Slink's the *snatch and grab*. Then we make a run for it. Clear?'

Lux nodded.

'Go.'

Lux ran from the warehouse, stopped at the first trailer and circled round it.

'OK.' Slink darted right and vanished behind the second trailer.

After a few moments, Lux reappeared and gave a thumbs-up.

Jack hurried over to her.

'The crew are all busy filming,' Lux whispered. 'I'll keep an eye out.'

'Thanks.' Jack jogged over to the second trailer, glanced around, then opened the door and stepped inside.

The man at the table looked up and rose to his feet when he saw Jack. He wore a tailored suit, had grey hair, a thin face and a pair of round glasses. 'Who are you?' He had a German accent.

Slink lowered himself down on a rope outside the main window. He used the sword to flip the catch, then pulled himself silently through.

Jack's eyes flitted to the laptop on the desk.

'You can't have it,' the grey-haired man said. He took a step forward, blocking Jack's view.

The bathroom door behind Slink opened and a large figure appeared.

Jack went to cry out, but it was too late – the man grabbed hold of Slink's arms.

'Get off me,' Slink shouted, kicking and squirming.

The grey-haired man removed his glasses and wiped them on his shirt. 'Nice try.'

CHAPTER EIGHT

JACK AND SLINK SAT ON A SOFA IN THE TRAILER, while the grey-haired man stood in front of them with his hands in his pockets and a look of mild amusement on his face.

The bodyguard was standing to one side, ready to grab the two Urban Outlaws should they make any sudden moves.

The grey-haired man's gaze settled on Jack. 'I assume you're the leader?' His German accent was mild. 'Who are you?'

Jack stared back at him. 'Who are *you*?'

'You may call me Leon.' He pursed his lips. 'Do I need to kill your friend here to get an answer?' His cold eyes flitted to Slink and back again.

Jack let out a breath. 'We are...freelance.'

Leon stared at him a moment longer. Then he broke into a booming laugh. He glanced at his bodyguard and said something in German.

He laughed too.

Leon composed himself and looked at Jack again. 'You are saying someone hired you?'

Jack shrugged.

'How did you get through security?'

Jack crossed his arms.

The man looked at the laptop on the desk and then back again. 'And what is your price?'

Jack hesitated. What was the point of keeping his mouth shut? If he did that for too long, Leon would probably make good on his threats and kill Slink. 'Plane tickets,' he said finally.

Leon's eyebrows rose. 'Tickets?'

'So we can go home.'

'United Kingdom?'

Jack nodded.

'Who is your employer?'

'I don't know.'

Leon sighed. 'You don't know or you don't want to tell me?'

Jack shrugged again. 'Bit of both.'

Leon considered him a moment and Jack knew he was trying to work out what to do with them.

It wasn't every day a couple of kids broke into your trailer and tried to steal a laptop from under you.

'Let him go and keep me,' Jack said, gesturing to Slink.

Leon pulled out a handkerchief from his pocket and dabbed his forehead. 'I don't think I can do that.'

'Who are you?' Slink said.

'You don't know?' Leon frowned. 'So, you were going to take from me, but...' His voice trailed off. 'You don't even know what is on the laptop, do you?'

'This is boring.' Slink stretched and yawned. 'You could just give it to us and save yourself a whole heap of trouble.'

'Trouble?' Leon said, a smile cracking his lips again. 'I don't think so.' He looked at Jack. 'I shall ask one more time, before things start to turn real nasty. Who. Are. You?'

'Someone with a lot of powerful friends.'

Leon inclined his head. 'And powerful enemies, I should guess.' He let out a long breath. 'I can see answers are going to be difficult.' He turned to his bodyguard. 'Pick one.'

The bodyguard snarled and pointed at Slink.

'Ah,' Leon said with a smile, 'the little one of the two. Weakest first?'

'I'm not weak,' Slink said, defiant.

'We shall see.'

There was a knock on the trailer door.

'Check it out.' Leon motioned for the bodyguard to answer it and pulled a pistol from his belt.

The bodyguard opened the door and stepped outside. He looked left and right. 'No one there.'

Suddenly a loop of rope dropped over his shoulders and pulled tight, pinning his arms against his body and yanking him backwards. The man's head slammed against the side of the trailer and he slumped.

A millisecond later, the side window of the trailer burst open as Lux erupted through it on the other end of the rope.

Glasses and mugs went flying in all directions, smashing against the walls.

Leon turned and Lux hit him square in the chest with both feet. As he stumbled backwards, Jack and Slink seized their chance and sprang forward, grabbing him.

Jack forced Leon's arm down, aiming the gun at the floor.

Lux grabbed a shard of broken glass and pressed it to the man's neck. 'Drop it.'

Leon snarled. 'Or what?'

Lux pushed the tip of the glass into his neck. 'I said *drop it*.'

Leon snorted his annoyance and the gun clattered to the floor.

Jack and Slink let go of him and stepped back.

'Lie down,' Lux breathed into Leon's ear.

Jack picked up a lamp, yanked the power cable from the wall and used it to tie Leon's hands together.

When he was sure Leon wasn't going anywhere for a while, he straightened up and looked at Lux. 'Well, that was pretty amazing.'

She winked. 'Thanks.'

'You're like a ninja,' Slink said. 'A cross between a ninja and' – he nodded at the shard of glass in her hand – 'a psychopathic stunt woman.'

'I think a ninja would be more stealthy than me, but I'll take it as a compliment.'

The bodyguard groaned.

Slink grabbed the rope and with Jack's help heaved the man on to the floor of the trailer.

As he tried to get up, Slink put a foot on his back and forced him to the floor. 'Stay still, sweetheart.'

Jack scooped up the laptop. 'Let's get out of here.'

They hurried from the trailer and ran between two sound studios.

At the end, they took a right and stopped outside a door.

Lux pulled a phone from her pocket and looked at it.

'Well?' Jack asked.

Before she spoke, Charlie stuck her head around the door. 'You're ten minutes late.' She stepped aside.

Jack tucked the laptop into his belt and covered it with his shirt before following Slink and Lux through.

'Sorry,' he said to Charlie. 'We ran into trouble. Did the tour guide notice we were gone?'

Charlie shook her head. 'No, thanks to Wren.'

They jogged along a corridor, then took a left and strode casually into the studio museum.

It was the last stop on the tour – a giant room filled with costumes and props from famous movies.

But Jack wasn't interested in them right now. He adjusted the laptop under his shirt and glanced around. 'Where's Wren? Is she OK?'

'She's fine.' Charlie pointed to the corner of the museum.

Wren was chatting away to the tour guide, but it was all one-sided. The poor guy looked exhausted.

Jack smiled.

They'd got away with it.

That wasn't a mission he'd forget any time soon.

• • •

Ten minutes later, Jack, Charlie, Slink, Wren and Lux met Drake and the SUV at the pre-arranged spot.

A screech of tyres made Jack glance towards the studio. A silver Mercedes erupted from a side road.

Jack spun back to the SUV. 'Let's go!' he shouted.

Everyone jumped in and Drake pulled away from the kerb.

The Mercedes accelerated after them in hot pursuit.

Drake shot across a main road and turned sharply down another side street. At the end, he took a left, then an immediate right, all the time with his foot hard to the floor, accelerating.

Jack glanced through the rear windscreen – the silver Mercedes was still following.

The SUV lurched as Drake turned left again.

The Mercedes pulled out of the side street, veered across the main road and swerved just in time to avoid an oncoming bus.

Ahead, cars queued at a set of traffic lights.

'Hold on.' Drake yanked the steering wheel hard over.

The SUV spun sideways, squeezed between two cars and bumped on to the kerb, taking out a metal bin and a lamp post.

'There goes the insurance excess.' Drake rammed his foot hard on the pedal, cutting across a coffee shop forecourt and a plaza. He leant on the horn and pedestrians jumped out of the way, diving in all directions.

The Mercedes tried the same manoeuvre, but side-swiped an oncoming car.

For a moment, Jack thought this would end the chase, but somehow the silver car kept coming – it too drove up on to the kerb and across the plaza after them.

Drake followed a wide pavement in front of the shops. More startled pedestrians leapt out of their path. One woman coming out of a clothes store, her arms laden with shopping bags, screamed and fell backwards through the entrance.

Slink laughed.

Drake zigzagged left and right, weaving between pedestrians. When he nearly hit an old man in a wheelchair, he said, 'I think it's time to get off here.'

He squeezed between two trees and managed to get the car back on to the correct side of the road.

Jack glanced through the rear window. By some miracle, the Mercedes was still on their tail.

Drake shook his head. 'What's on that laptop that they want so badly?'

Jack tensed. 'No idea.'

They shot across an intersection.

Wheels screeched and horns sounded.

Suddenly, there was a huge smashing sound.

The Mercedes had driven straight into the side of a pickup truck, slamming it into a van.

Two more cars smashed into the van, and Jack winced.

People started climbing out of their vehicles and waving their fists at the occupants of the silver car.

Jack looked forward again.

Drake reduced the car to a normal speed. 'Well,' he said, 'that was fun.'

Wren leant forward between the seats with a look of awe and said to Drake, 'Will you adopt me?'

Jack let out a slow breath. Now they could get back to New York and...what? he thought. Go home? They'd heard nothing from Obi, which meant there was still no sign of Hector.

Wren laughed.

Jack turned in his seat to see Slink pulling out two of the inflatable people from under his hoodie. 'Slink.'

'What?' Slink said. 'They were being thrown out.'

Jack shook his head and looked at the laptop in his hands. They might have won this mission, but it seemed they had lost the main one – to stop Hector.

• • •

The Urban Outlaws had just got back to Serene's loft in New York when there was a beeping sound.

All heads turned to the office. The computer screen was flashing red.

'No way,' Obi breathed.

'What?' Jack said.

'The camera at Hector's apartment – it's detected movement.'

They all rushed into the office and gathered around Obi as he brought up an image of the apartment.

Obi was right – standing inside and just closing the door was Cloud, the slim woman who worked for Hector.

Jack spun to Drake. 'Can you get us there *fast*?'

'Give me a few minutes.' Drake hurried down the spiral staircase.

Charlie ran to the gadget room and returned seconds later with a few items.

She handed Jack a leather wallet, thirty centimetres square and five thick. He undid the clasps and opened the flap. Inside was a rugged tablet PC.

'Obi,' Charlie said, 'would you please link the camera to the tablet?'

Obi did as she instructed and an image of the apartment appeared on the screen in Jack's hand. 'Thanks,' he said.

Now he could watch what Cloud was doing as they made their way back there.

Charlie then handed Jack and Slink a mobile phone, headset and a micro-camera each. 'You can fit these cameras under your clothes and Obi will be able to see everything.'

Slink reached under his hoodie and pressed the camera to it. It made a small hole in the fabric and an image of the room appeared on the monitor.

'I want you and Wren to wait here with Obi,' Jack said, fitting his own camera and headset.

'Are you sure?' Charlie said.

'Too many of us will draw attention. We're just going to follow Cloud for now. See where she goes. Hopefully she'll lead us straight to Hector.'

'What about me?' Lux said.

'You know the area – we could use you.'

Jack, Slink and Lux marched to the spiral staircase and rushed down it.

Outside the shop, Drake pulled to the kerb in a pizza delivery van.

'Don't ask,' he said as they hopped in. 'It's all I could get at such short notice.'

Slink laughed.

• • •

As they drove out of Chinatown towards Central Park, Jack sat in the passenger seat and looked at the screen in his lap. The view of the apartment was clear and he could see Cloud kneeling by the front door beside an open cupboard, picking up items and putting them into a duffel bag.

Jack clenched his teeth and looked up from the screen. 'How long until we're there?'

'About ten minutes,' Drake said, turning down a side road and weaving between two parked trucks.

'We're not going to get there in time.' Jack looked at the screen again.

Cloud finished putting the objects in her bag, then closed the door to the cupboard and straightened up. To Jack's relief, rather than leaving the apartment straight away, she started walking slowly around, checking under furniture and inside drawers and cupboards.

Good, he thought. That bought them some more time.

Cloud was obviously making sure there were no signs that they'd been there and that they'd left nothing lying around.

Jack kept his eyes glued to the screen and the next five minutes passed in anxious silence.

On the screen he watched Cloud find the origami chewing gum wrapper under the bedside table and shove it into her duffel bag. She then glanced around each room one more time and finally left the apartment.

Jack closed the screen and slid it under the seat. 'We won't be needing that any more.' They were still at least five minutes away.

Slink said, 'What are we going to do?'

Jack ran a quick scenario through his head – Cloud waiting for a lift, getting in, going down to the lobby.

'We're not giving up yet,' Drake said, beeping the horn, putting his foot to the floor and overtaking two cars.

Jack had a flashback of the car chase in Hollywood, but at this speed they might actually make it to the apartment in time.

The following minutes dragged like hours.

He kept looking at the clock on the van's dashboard. Its second light seemed to be blinking on and off way too slowly.

Finally Drake turned on to Fifth Avenue and Jack leant forward in his seat. Up ahead, he could see the apartment building. He pointed through the windscreen. 'There she is.'

Cloud came out of the front doors and got into a waiting yellow taxi.

'Is that her?' Lux said. 'In that cab?'

'Yes.'

Drake jammed his foot hard to the floor. The van's engine revved and he overtook another taxi. The driver beeped his horn and made a rude gesture through the windscreen.

Drake focused on the taxi ahead, and when they were a couple of cars back he slowed, keeping a safe distance so as not to be spotted.

Jack could make out the back of Cloud's head in the rear seat.

The taxi turned right and then, a few roads down, right again.

'She must be going somewhere in Lower Manhattan,' Lux said.

'What's there?' Jack asked.

Lux's eyebrows rose and she glanced at him. 'Everything. Wall Street – the main business district. She could be going anywhere.'

Jack just wanted to get to Hector and stop him before he did even more damage, before he set up more hackers and stole secrets.

Every traffic light and junction seemed to be against them. Several times, Slink offered to get out of the car, run over to the taxi, drag Cloud from it and demand answers.

Jack assured him that this wasn't the best idea because they didn't want to draw the attention of the police, or of Hector. Noble would be in danger if he suspected that they were hot on his heels.

Eventually the taxi stopped. Set some way back from the road was a large square red-brick building, thirteen storeys high.

Slink leant forward in his seat. 'What is this place?'

Jack pointed at a sign that read, 'Welcome to Police Headquarters.'

'This is One Police Plaza,' Lux said. 'What's she doing here?'

They watched as Cloud got out, said something to the driver and then strode up the path.

'Well,' Drake said, 'there's no way we can follow her. There have to be a thousand cops in there.'

Jack stared at Cloud as she headed towards the building. 'Don't be so sure,' he said quietly, his mind racing.

Slink grinned at Drake.

Jack scooped the tablet PC from under the seat, switched it on and pressed a finger to his ear. 'Obi?'

'Here.'

'Are you still picking up our body cameras?'

'Yeah, I can see.'

'Good. In that case, could you patch me directly into Serene's computer?' Jack turned to face Slink. 'Take this and follow her.' He leant over, picked up an empty pizza box from the seat next to Slink and shoved it into his hands. 'Go. Quick.'

Slink pulled the Yankees baseball cap low over his eyes and opened the door.

Serene's desktop appeared on the tablet in front of Jack. He now had remote access. He opened a dialog box and set to work.

'What are you doing?' Lux said.

Jack glanced at Slink hurrying after Cloud, then looked back at the tablet screen. 'Trying to get into their system.'

'Whose system?'

Jack kept his eyes on the screen and nodded at the red-brick building to their left.

Lux gasped. 'Wait – you're hacking into the police headquarters?'

'Yep.' Jack's fingers worked fast, moving in a blur as he typed. First of all he located the main servers. The next task was to get into them.

Serene had some useful built-in hacking tools, but none of them was up to the job.

Jack took a calming breath.

This was down to him.

'Obi,' he said into his headset, 'can you help me out and make sure our track is well hidden? I can't do it all at once.'

The police's network security was among the best he'd ever seen, but not good enough. Jack spotted a way to circumvent it.

The challenge was not to get caught.

'Anyone noticed yet?' he asked.

'We've just checked,' Charlie said. 'You're clear. No one's tracing you.'

Obi brought up a small window on Jack's screen – it showed the view from Slink's hidden camera.

He was now walking through the visitor's entrance to One Police Plaza.

Up ahead, Cloud showed her ID and passed through the metal detectors.

Slink slowed his pace. 'Jack?'

'I'm working on it,' Jack said. 'Stall. I need more time.'

Slink knelt and pretended to tie his shoelaces.

'Jack,' Obi said in his ear, 'someone's realised you're trying to hack into the system and they've started a trace.'

'How long?' Jack said, typing faster than ever. So far he'd worked out half of the code.

'A minute,' Obi said, 'maybe less.'

Jack's eyes flitted to Slink's camera view.

At the other end of the lobby, beyond a set of security barriers, Cloud was standing with five or six other people, waiting for a lift.

A guard stepped into view and looked directly at Slink and beckoned him forward. 'Who's the pizza for, kid?'

Slink walked towards him, slowly. 'Erm...'

'I'm working on it,' Jack muttered. Three-quarters of the code was done. His mind and fingers now worked in fluid harmony.

'They're nearly on to you,' Obi said. 'Ten seconds at the most.'

A screen flashed up and Jack was into the police computers. *Yes!* He quickly navigated to the personnel section.

The guard frowned at Slink. 'Well, what's the name?'

'Erm...'

'Five seconds, Jack,' Obi said.

Jack opened the first file and scanned down a list of names, but none of them seemed to work in the building itself.

'Four...'

The guard took a step towards Slink. 'Kid?'

'Three...'

'Come on,' Jack muttered, his eyes continuing down the list of names. Most of them were traffic cops.

'Two...'

The guard touched the radio at his hip.

Jack finally found a name of someone who worked inside the building. 'Lieutenant Fredericks,' he said into the microphone. 'Kenny Fredericks.' He quickly closed the connection.

'Kenny Fredericks,' Slink blurted out.

The guard stared at him a moment. 'OK. Come on.'

Slink let out an audible breath.

'Traced?' Jack asked Obi.

'No. It was close though.'

Slink walked through the metal detector and it beeped.

Jack tensed.

The guard grabbed a wand from the side and waved it over the pizza box, then over Slink.

It beeped too.

The screen in Jack's lap went dark.

CHAPTER NINE

JACK LIFTED UP THE TABLET SCREEN AND STARED at it. 'What's going on?' he said.

'Chill.' Charlie's voice came through the earpiece. 'It's OK. I reckon Slink's just pulled the phone out of his pocket. That's why you've lost the image. He would've disconnected the camera and headset.'

'What does that mean?' Lux said.

'He's showing the guard his phone,' Jack replied, relaxing a little. 'Hopefully that'll be enough and he won't find the camera and wires.'

They waited in silence.

The minutes dragged.

A couple of police officers glanced into the van as they passed.

Jack couldn't take much more. He reached for the door handle and was about to go after Slink when the camera view snapped back on.

Slink was entering the lift with Cloud and five other people.

Jack let out a sigh of relief. 'Thank God.'

Cloud stayed near the doors, while Slink, keeping his eyes down, made for the back corner.

'Good work,' Jack breathed into the headset.

The lift went up several floors and Cloud got out.

Just as the doors were about to shut, Slink snuck through and stood in the hallway, with the pizza box held in front of him.

He pretended to check for the correct name and room number as Cloud walked a few doors along and knocked.

There was a muffled reply and she entered.

Slink tucked the box under his arm, jogged to the same door and pressed his ear against it.

'What can you hear?' Jack said.

'Voices,' Slink murmured. He looked up and down the hallway, then pressed his ear back to the door. A couple of seconds later he pulled back. 'Can't make out what they're saying,' he whispered.

Jack leant in to the display. The name on the door said, 'Chief of Staff, D.B. Whitaker.'

'Chief of staff?' Lux said, incredulous.

Jack looked at her. 'What does that mean?'

'Second highest job in NYPD,' Drake said.

Jack frowned at the screen. What was Cloud doing visiting him?

'What should I do?' Slink whispered.

'Next door down,' Jack said.

Slink hurried to the door and knocked softly.

There was no answer, so he opened the door and peered inside.

The office was empty, so he snuck in.

Jack smiled to himself as he spotted a connecting door in the side wall. 'To your right, Slink.'

Slink tossed the pizza box on to the desk, hurried over to the door and pressed an ear to it.

A few seconds later, he pulled back again. 'Still can't hear a word,' he hissed.

'Lie on the floor,' Charlie said.

'Huh?'

'Next to the door, Slink. Lie on the ground.'

Slink did as he was told and the camera view dropped.

'Follow my instructions carefully,' Charlie said. 'Take off your headset and push the microphone under the door. Then listen to the earpiece. I'm going to record the sound the microphone picks up, but I'm also going to delay playing it back to your earpiece by a second or two, to avoid feedback. Understand?'

'No,' Slink breathed. He took off his headset, slid the microphone under the door, then turned on his side.

A couple of seconds later, the voices came through everyone's earpieces loud and clear.

'... know any other way I can help you with that,' a man's voice said.

That must be the chief, Jack thought.

'David...' Cloud said, in a soft voice. She had a posh accent. 'You promised that you would ensure the police stayed away.'

'I know. And you promised we'd correspond only by email. Look how that worked out.'

'My employer has been more than generous over the years. If it wasn't for him –'

'I'm aware of everything he's done for me,' the chief said, sounding agitated yet under control, 'and I appreciate it. I really do. And that's why I've returned most of those favours. I just can't see how –'

'I've been instructed to tell you that another three hundred thousand is waiting to be transferred to your account. All it needs is our final authorisation.'

There was a short pause and the chief sighed. 'I'll see what I can do.'

'Thank you.'

There was the sound of heeled shoes on a wooden floor, then a scraping. 'Oh, and David?'

'Yes?'

'Thank you for sorting out that little problem when we first arrived.'

A door opened and closed.

Slink pulled the microphone back, leapt to his feet and grabbed the pizza box. He opened the door to the hallway, peered out and watched Cloud as she stepped into the lift.

'Go back,' Jack said.

Slink pulled into the office again. 'What?'

'Look around a moment. Do it slowly.'

The camera view panned across the room and Jack's eyes soaked up every detail of the office – pictures, filing cabinets, the air conditioning vent, the windows.

'OK. Done.'

Slink slipped into the hallway and closed the door behind him.

As he hurried back to the lift, Jack's eyes scanned the walls and ceiling. There were cameras, heat sensors, smoke alarms...

Slink hit the button for the lift.

Jack leant back in his seat and let out a slow breath.

'Well?' Lux said. 'What was all that about?'

'No idea, but we need to find out.'

• • •

A few minutes later, Slink hopped into the van and Drake pulled away from the kerb, following Cloud in the taxi again.

It took a left and waited at a red light.

'Where's she going now?' Slink said.

'Looks like they're heading to Brooklyn,' Drake replied.

Sure enough, they were soon driving across the Brooklyn Bridge.

Slink leant forward and looked at the river on either side. 'What's in this Brooklyn place?'

Drake gripped the steering wheel. 'Could be anything.'

When they reached the other side of the bridge, they turned right, travelled for another five minutes or so and eventually stopped next to a pontoon that jutted out into the river.

Cloud stepped from the taxi, dropped a duffel bag into a bin, then strode along the pontoon to a waiting speedboat.

Jack leant forward in his seat and squinted at the giant man standing behind the wheel of the boat. 'That's Monday.'

Cloud got on board.

'They're getting away.' Slink went to climb out of the van, but Jack stopped him. 'What are you doing?'

'They'll see us,' Jack said.

'So?'

'We'll lose the element of surprise.'

They watched as Monday turned the boat around and sped away.

When they were out of sight, Jack got out of the van and hurried over to the bin. He glanced around, then reached inside and pulled out Cloud's bag.

He hurried back to the van and climbed in.

'What's in it?' Lux said.

Jack opened the bag. Inside was the circuit board and other parts from the apartment. In the bottom were bits of paper, some screwed up, some torn and tatty. He showed the others.

'Great,' Slink said. 'She's left a load of rubbish.'

'Maybe we can get something from all this,' Jack said.

'I can tell you exactly what you'll get from that,' Slink said. 'A freakin disease.'

Jack pulled out one of the pieces of paper and examined it. 'It's a delivery note.' He held it up to his hidden camera. 'Charlie, you getting this?'

'Yeah, I see it. It's for Bluconn processors. Fifty of them.'

'*Fifty?*' Slink said. 'Why would Hector want fifty processors?'

'They're high-end too,' Charlie said. 'They would've cost a lot of money.'

Jack's eyes moved over the other scraps of paper in the bag and he sighed. They'd been so close to finding Hector and now he'd slipped through their fingers again.

It was so frustrating.

No, it was beyond that – it was *infuriating*.

Jack balled his fists. Now all they had to go on was a bag filled with rubbish. The only other – He snapped his fingers.

'What is it?' Drake said, glancing around.

Jack yanked the tablet PC from under the seat and connected to Serene's computer again.

'What are you doing, Jack?' Charlie said in his ear.

'I'm hacking into that D.B. Whitaker guy's computer. I need to see if there are any clues to where Hector is hiding out.'

'Are you nuts?' Obi said. 'They'll definitely trace us this time. They'll be on alert after the last attack.'

'Not if I'm fast enough.' Jack flexed his fingers, took a quick breath and set to work.

He was relieved to see the police network engineers hadn't had time to change their security yet. They were probably still scratching their heads, wondering —

'Jack,' Obi said. 'They're on to you.'

'Already?' Jack navigated to the main email system and scanned down the addresses.

'You've got ten seconds.'

Jack's eyes moved down the list. 'Come *on*.'

Finally he found Chief Whitaker's stored emails and opened the folder.

'Five seconds,' Obi said.

'Jack,' Charlie said, sounding agitated, 'we can't get Serene into trouble. If they trace the signal here –'

'I know.' Jack moved down the emails, looking for any that might be from either Cloud or Hector. 'I need a few more seconds.'

'You don't have a few seconds,' Charlie said.

Jack's gaze locked on to an email from 'CACloud90046'.

'*Jack*.'

He went to click on it, but the screen vanished. 'What the...?' He tried reconnecting, but it was useless – the connection was dead. 'What's happened?'

'I pulled the plug,' Charlie said in a quiet voice.

'You did what?'

'I disconnected the line,' Charlie said. 'They were about to trace us.'

'That's just great.' Jack threw the tablet into the footwell. Then he took a deep breath, composing himself. He glanced at the others. 'Sorry.' He adjusted his mic. 'Sorry, Charlie. I didn't mean to snap at you.' She'd just been watching his back, and she was right – they couldn't risk getting Serene into trouble. Not with everything she'd done for them.

'It's OK, I understand,' Charlie said. 'I want to get to Hector too, remember?'

'I know.' Jack looked at Drake. 'Could you please take us back to the loft?'

'What are we doing now?' Slink said as they pulled from the kerb.

'The only option we've got left,' Jack said.

'What's that?' Lux asked.

Jack stared out of the window. 'We're going to break in to New York City's police headquarters.'

• • •

Jack, Slink, Lux and Drake walked into Serene's loft.

Charlie was sitting at the dining table, waiting for them.

'Mind having a look at what we've got?' Jack said, striding towards the gadget room.

As he walked past the office, Jack saw Obi and Wren sitting in front of the computer. He stopped.

'It looks like a normal plane hangar from above,' he was saying to her in a hushed voice, 'but underground there are at least ten more levels.'

Jack looked at the monitor in front of them. It showed a satellite image of some kind of airfield in a desert.

'And there's aliens down there?' Wren said, her eyes wide.

'Yeah.' Obi clicked the mouse and brought up a black-and-white photo of a grey alien on an autopsy table. 'The American government have seven of them down there,' he said, as if stating a fact. 'Five are dead – they have them frozen – but the other two are alive.' He glanced at Wren. 'Where do you think all our technology comes from?'

That was all Jack could take. He cleared his throat. They jumped.

'What are you two doing?'

'I'm teaching Wren stuff,' Obi said.

Jack's eyebrows rose. 'Teaching her what?'

Wren straightened in her chair. 'American history.'

Jack rolled his eyes and pointed at the screen. 'How is *that* history?'

Obi opened his mouth to answer, but Jack cut across him, 'Come on, I need you two to help with this,' and he went into the gadget room.

Once everyone was gathered around the Think Desk, Jack unzipped the bag and upended it.

'What's all that?' Wren said.

'Clues.' Jack held up a couple of receipts. 'We need to organise these so we can work out what Hector's been up to.'

Charlie waved her hand over the desk and it sprung to life. She took one of the pieces of paper and pressed it face down on the surface. There was a soft beep, and when she lifted the receipt away, there was a perfect copy underneath it.

Charlie then tapped on the digital copy of the receipt and moved it around the display.

'This is a giant screen?' Slink said, stepping back and looking underneath it.

'Yes,' Charlie said. 'And a scanner. And a computer. Serene showed me – you can copy everything digitally.'

'It's awesome.' Wren leant over, touched the corner of the digital receipt and spun it around.

Jack turned back to the Think Desk. 'OK,' he said. 'Let's scan all this stuff.'

Within a few minutes it was done – every receipt and scrap of paper was scanned into the Think Desk.

'Wow, yeah, really great,' Slink said, frowning at it all. 'Now we've got a load of digital rubbish too.'

'Not rubbish.' Jack reached over, dragged a sketch of a circuit diagram towards him and spun it the right way up. 'Charlie?'

'Looks like some kind of mainboard.' She glanced at the other pieces. 'Wait, look at this.' She dragged over a receipt for memory sticks and another sketch of what appeared to be a network of some kind. She put the three next to each other.

'What is it?' Lux asked.

'Looks like Hector's had another custom board made.'

'What for?'

Charlie's eyebrows knitted together. 'I don't know yet.'

Jack stared at the display a while, then motioned for the others to leave Charlie to it. This had now turned into a technical issue – something that only Charlie could understand – clues that only she could put together, and, right now, he had a mission to plan.

As they all left the room, Jack glanced back at Charlie and he was glad they had someone as clever as her on their side.

As they walked into the main room he said to Obi, 'We need everything you can get on the police building.'

'I can help,' Lux offered, joining them. 'This is what I do.'

'You can get us a plan of the building?' Jack asked her.

'Leave it to me.' She went into the office, sat down and started typing.

'I'm hungry,' Obi said.

'Me too,' Wren said.

'Me three,' Slink added and they went to the kitchen and started opening cupboards.

'I'll help,' Drake said.

Wren smiled. 'Can you cook?'

'I'm great at burning things.'

As they prepared dinner, Drake said, 'So are you guys homeless?'

'We're not homeless,' Wren said. 'We live in a bunker.'

Drake's eyebrows rose. 'A bunker? Under London?'

'Yep.'

'How did you find that?'

'Noble gave it to us,' Slink said. 'He also funded us in the early days. We look after ourselves now though.'

Drake nodded. 'And how did you get so good at all that free-running stuff?'

Slink started peeling potatoes. 'A few years back, when I still lived with my mum, we had, like, no money. She was always missing the rent and the landlord was this really nasty guy. Every time I went to school, he'd corner me and threaten us with eviction. So eventually I had to start climbing out of the window. I taught myself parkour because I had no choice really.'

Drake took the potatoes from him and cut them up. 'Wasn't that dangerous?'

Slink shrugged. 'Guess so. Mum didn't like it, but she quickly realised she had no way to stop me.' He wiped his hands on a kitchen towel. 'So whenever she needed something – like food or medicine – I'd climb out of the window, shimmy along the ledge, then jump across to the roof of the block of flats next door and drop down behind it.' He looked at the clock on the wall. 'That reminds me – I need to call her and see how she's doing.'

Jack leant against the wall and watched them, though he wasn't really paying attention – he was trying to work out how they would break in to One Police Plaza.

It was no good trying to hack into their computer systems – they'd be on high alert now. And they were unlikely to fall for the pizza delivery trick again. Besides, Slink had got past that guard and the barrier easily enough, but that was during the day. To get a good look at Chief Whitaker's computer, they'd have to go at night. That also meant a more physical approach was needed.

Charlie shouted, breaking Jack out of his thoughts. He looked over at her.

'I've got it,' she said. 'I know what Hector's done.'

Jack hurried into the gadget room as Charlie stepped back from the Think Desk with a look of utter excitement on her face. She pointed at the display. She had linked and arranged most of the scrap bits of paper.

'That was quick,' Jack said, his eyes roaming over everything. 'What is it?' To him, it still looked like nonsense.

'A computer.'

Jack cocked an eyebrow. 'That's all?'

Charlie reached to the corners of the Think Desk and brought her hands together. The image shrank, revealing a sophisticated technical blueprint. 'This,' she said, waving a finger at the image, 'is a custom, one-of-a-kind computer.'

'Like Proteus?' he asked.

Proteus was a quantum computer they'd destroyed. It was what had started all of this mess with Hector and his father.

'No,' Charlie said. 'This is way more basic than that, but it's still sophisticated.'

'So' – Jack frowned – 'what's it for then?'

'Hector needed something specifically to hold the modified virus, the program he's now using as a hacking tool, right?' Charlie took a breath. 'He needed something that could contain it. Bring it under his control. This' – she tapped the display – 'this is it. We destroy this, and Hector has nothing.'

• • •

Jack and Charlie spent the next thirty minutes trying to work out if the computer Hector had built had any weaknesses.

Charlie finally pointed at another part of the circuit diagram. 'It has several lines out to the internet and a sophisticated firewall system. I've checked – there's no way in without Hector knowing.'

'And if that happens,' Jack said, 'he'll know we're in New York.' Their only advantage – the element of surprise – would be gone. 'We have to destroy the hardware and the program directly somehow,' Jack continued.

'That's not going to be easy though,' Charlie said. 'We still have no idea where Hector is.'

Jack glanced over at the office. 'We're working on it.'

• • •

After they'd all eaten an interesting meal of corn dogs, mashed potato and pancakes, Lux called Jack into the office.

Stomach churning in protest, Jack pushed his plate away, rose from the dining table and went to see what she had.

She brought up an architectural drawing of the police headquarters.

'That's great.' Jack was impressed by the level of detail – the plan had everything, all the way down to individual power conduits.

Lux smiled at him. 'I can send it to the Think Desk if you want.'

Jack straightened up. 'Thanks.' He walked back to the gadget room and Charlie joined him.

She moved Hector's computer diagram aside and pulled up the plan of the building.

Jack leant over the Think Desk and studied it. As the seconds passed, he felt an awful sense of failure.

'What's wrong?' Charlie said, noticing his pained expression.

'We have a problem. Obi?' he called. 'When you're done eating, can you see if you can get into their security?'

'I don't think you'll be able to,' Lux said as she came into the gadget room.

'What do you mean?' Charlie said.

'I looked – it's on an isolated system.'

'Where's the control room?' Jack said. 'It's not on this plan.'

'Underneath the main building,' Lux said. 'There's no other way in or out.'

'OK.' Jack focused on the plan of the building again. 'We'll go in via the roof.'

'No good either,' Lux said. 'They have six cameras, each covering the other. No way I can see how to get past them.'

'*Six?*' Charlie said, incredulous. 'They really mean business, don't they?'

Jack turned from the desk.

All they wanted to do was take a quick look at Chief Whitaker's emails. Why was that so hard?

Then he reminded himself – they were dealing with a high-ranking police official.

Obi, Slink, Wren and Drake walked into the room.

'What's up, buttercups?' Slink said, looking around at the depressed faces.

Lux forced a smile at him.

'We're trying to work out how to break in to the police building,' Charlie said.

'I've already done it,' Slink said. 'I can just do it again. It was easy.'

Jack shook his head. 'It won't be this time. They would've seen my attack on their systems and stepped up the building's security.'

'They'll be on alert,' Lux said. 'They'll think it's terrorists.'

Jack nodded. Another stupid mistake he'd made. He was starting to make a habit of them.

'Cheer up, Jack.' Slink leant against the glass wall. 'You'll work out a way. You always do.'

Slink was right – instead of moping about past mistakes, Jack needed to learn from them and move forward. They were so close to Hector. Just a few more clues and they'd have him.

He turned back to the plan. There had to be a way inside without being shot by the police SWAT teams.

He closed his eyes and remembered the office next door to Chief Whitaker's: there were no cameras or sensors inside, just in the main hallway, which meant –

Now, eyes wide open, Jack zoomed the plan in on the window to that same office. 'The only way is going to be through this.'

'The window doesn't open,' Lux said. 'It's solid, reinforced glass. Triple-layered. It would take forever to cut through it. No way you could do that.'

'There might be one way.' Charlie was staring across the room.

Jack followed her gaze to the back wall where the crate was sitting.

Charlie nodded at it. 'We could use that.'

'Wait a minute,' Jack said, realising what Charlie was getting at. 'You can use that from another street, right?'

'Yes.'

'In that case,' Jack turned back to the Think Desk, 'we have the beginnings of a crazy plan.'

'Cool beans.' Slink slapped his hands together. 'I love me some crazy.'

CHAPTER TEN

AT SUNSET, JACK AND LUX WERE SITTING ON the roof of a building two blocks down from One Police Plaza…and Jack hated it. Being twenty floors up, perched on the edge of a building was his idea of a complete nightmare. But, right at that moment, it was marginally less scary than what would happen if they let Hector continue with his plans.

Jack had a telescope on a small tripod in front of him and through it he had a clear view of the surrounding area.

After making sure no one had spotted them, he pressed a finger to his ear. 'Obi, how are we doing?'

'I'm patched in to all the surrounding traffic and CCTV cameras in the area. So far it's quiet.'

'OK.' Jack took a deep breath. One false move and they'd have the entire New York's Police Department after them. 'Let's do this.'

'Moving into position,' Charlie said.

Jack swung the telescope around and watched as Serene's laundry van turned into a road a few streets away and parked at the kerb. Drake had removed the labels so it was now just a plain white van.

Drake and Charlie hopped out.

They were both wearing overalls and hard hats. Drake quickly set up an orange tent next to the van, while Charlie opened a side door, grabbed a coil of thick cable and unrolled it.

Drake took one end of the cable into the tent and re-emerged a few minutes later.

'Ready when you are, Jack,' Charlie said, as they clambered back into the van.

Jack moved the telescope so he was watching a tower block across the road from Drake and Charlie. There was nothing remarkable about it – just a rectangular column of concrete and glass.

No, the problem was at the base.

There was a small convenience store and, through the window, Jack could make out the shopkeeper sitting behind the counter.

As soon as Drake and Charlie opened the rear doors of the van, he'd see what they were doing and call the police.

Jack had spent a long time trying to work out alternative locations for the laundry van, but had come up empty. This was the only place they could use – the safest distance away, out of view of the police.

Considering this was one of the busiest cities in the world – that had been no mean feat.

This was also where Wren had come up with a brilliant idea.

'You're up, Wren,' Jack whispered.

She appeared from around the corner and hurried towards the shop.

'Jack,' Lux whispered, 'are you sure she can do this on her own?'

He smiled. 'Just watch this.'

Jack had learned quite a while ago that Wren's cute appearance was deceptive.

Wren entered the shop and walked along one of the aisles. She picked up a packet of biscuits, glanced around, then made a big show of shoving them under her hoodie.

The shopkeeper stood, his eyes fixed on her.

Wren moved to another shelf, grabbed a giant bag of sweets and stuffed them under her hoodie too.

She then made a beeline for the door.

The shopkeeper stepped in front of her. 'Not so fast, kid.'

Wren went to step around the guy, but he grabbed her shoulders.

'Get off.' As Wren struggled, the packet of biscuits fell to the floor, followed by the sweets.

The shopkeeper snarled. 'Got you.'

Suddenly Wren twisted around, there was a clicking sound, and the man staggered back in surprise.

A set of handcuffs now secured his wrists together behind him.

Not wasting a second, Wren dropped to the floor, there was another clicking sound and she straightened up again.

The shopkeeper went to take a step back, but a pair of metal cuffs now bound his ankles too.

Wren lunged forward, knocking him off-balance, and he crashed to the floor.

With another swift movement, she pressed a piece of tape over the guy's mouth.

She stepped back and winced. 'Sorry. I won't hurt you. It's life or death,' she assured him.

She then glanced out of the shop window, locked the door and turned out the lights. 'Done.'

Jack glanced over at Lux – she looked stunned by what had just happened.

'Brilliant, Wren,' Jack said into the mic.

'Thanks.'

Jack turned his attention back to their target building – One Police Plaza.

'How you doing, Slink?'

'All gravy.'

'There.' Lux pointed.

Slink's silhouette ran along the roof of a low adjoining building and leapt up on to another. Once on the far side, he stopped.

Jack and Lux scanned the area – no one had noticed him.

In front of Slink, the police building jutted out, supported by rectangular concrete columns that hung above his head. He'd have to jump across to them.

Jack pulled out a laptop and an image popped up on the screen. Jack and Lux could now see the world from Slink's point of view.

Slink slipped off his jacket and chucked it on to the roof behind him. He was wearing the military exoskeleton from Serene's gadget room. Charlie had modified it for the task, shortening it and improving the hand grippers.

'Wish me luck,' Slink whispered.

He took a few steps back, crouched down, then ran forward and launched himself off the edge of the roof. He sailed across the gap, gripped the sides of a concrete column and hauled himself up.

'Nice one,' Jack said.

When Slink reached the top, he grabbed either side of the first window and continued upward like a mechanical beetle.

Slink was soon halfway up the building's facade and still climbing at a fast rate.

Jack and Lux gave the area another scan.

The entrance to One Police Plaza was on the other face of the building – cops came and went, but none of them could see Slink from their viewpoint.

Jack moved the telescope back to the foyer of the building opposite Drake and Charlie.

The window was still dark and he could just make out Wren standing by the door.

'Two more floors,' Slink said.

Jack swung the telescope back to the police headquarters and watched as Slink climbed the last few metres and stopped at the target window.

He reached down to his feet and locked them on – keeping him gripped to the window. Then, with his hands now free, Slink unclipped a cylinder from his hip.

He tugged out a suction cup attached to one end and stuck it to the middle of the window. Once it was secure, Slink pulled a set of diamond cutters mounted on arms from the other end of the cylinder.

It had only taken Charlie an hour or so to make the device, and Jack couldn't help but be impressed by its simple yet clever design. 'All right, Slink, get clear of it.'

Now for the real tricky part – they needed power. A *lot* of power.

Slink reached down, re-engaged his exoskeleton legs, then shimmied sideways like a crab.

When Slink was several windows to the left, Jack moved the telescope to the laundry van. 'OK, Charlie. This is your bit.'

The rear van doors opened, revealing the Stinger mounted in the back. Jack could make out the thick wire that snaked through the side door and over to the tent on the pavement next to it.

Charlie and Drake had set up the tent, opened up a manhole cover and connected the Stinger to the main power supply beneath the street.

They now had all the juice they needed.

'Everyone, brace yourselves,' Charlie said, gripping the sides of the Stinger and aiming it between the buildings. 'Three, two, one...'

A pair of harpoons shot through the air and hit the brickwork next to the window.

Slink shimmied over to it, connected the two wires to the cylinder, and got back out of the way. 'Do it.'

Charlie hit a button on the side of the Stinger.

There was a faint crackling sound and the diamond cutters started to spin.

Jack could just make out a faint wisp of smoke as the diamonds cut the glass. 'It's working.' His grip tightened on the telescope.

Thirty seconds later, more smoke wafted into the air.

'Slink?' Jack said.

'Just a little further.'

Another twenty seconds passed before Slink finally said, 'I think that's it.'

Jack could see the arms of the cutters were glowing red hot.

Charlie cut the power. 'Safe.'

Slink moved back to the window and severed both the wires.

Charlie spooled them back into the Stinger and she pulled the doors of the van closed.

Jack let out a breath. 'Well?' he said, refocusing on Slink. 'Is it definitely through?'

Careful not to burn himself, Slink removed the cylinder and reattached it to another part of the window, out of the way. Then he reached up and pressed the centre of the glass.

Nothing happened.

Slink braced his feet and tried again. 'It's moving...'

After a few more seconds, there was a heavy *thunk* as it fell inside.

'Yes,' Slink said.

Jack punched the air. He couldn't believe it – their plan was working.

Slink gripped the hole and pulled himself into the office.

Jack looked at Slink's camera view on the laptop. 'Next door – *the computer*.'

Slink opened the connecting door and hurried into the Chief's office. He stepped over to the desk and disconnected the computer's keyboard, mouse and display. Then he pulled out a small black box from his pocket and connected it to the USB port.

Jack unfolded a laptop in front of him. Charlie had fixed another black box with an antenna on to it.

He clicked an icon on the desktop and a window sprang up.

He was now linked wirelessly to Chief Whitaker's computer. A password box appeared.

'I'm in.'

'Err, Jack?'

Jack glanced at Lux. 'What?'

She pointed.

There was thick smoke coming from the office next door to Slink. 'What the −?' He grabbed the telescope and saw that, much to his horror, smoke was now filling the room.

Before Jack had time to react, an alarm sounded.

For a few seconds his mind refused to function and he just stared helplessly.

There were no cameras or sensors in the offices, but there were smoke detectors − something he hadn't expected to cause them any problems.

The alarm pierced the night.

Suddenly sprinklers turned on in the ceiling, dousing the rooms in water.

'What's going on?' Slink rushed back to the connecting door. 'No way − the glass has set fire to the carpet.'

Jack's mind raced – the people who worked in the building wouldn't go to investigate the fire – that was the fire brigade's job. No, they would have to evacuate and wait for them to arrive.

As if on cue, fire engine sirens blared in the distance.

'We have to be quick.' Jack executed his program and in less than ten seconds it had cracked into the system.

There wasn't time to check the main computer's documents, so he went straight for Chief Whitaker's emails again.

His eyes scanned through the list until he found the one from CACloud90046.

'Well?' Lux said.

'Cloud,' he muttered. He opened it and read the short message:

Island agreed. Notify when secured.

Jack went to the Sent folder and found a message sent from the Chief ten minutes later.

The heading was 'FBI Training'.

Lux frowned at the screen. 'FBI Training?'

Jack opened the email and, as he read, confusion gave way to relief. This was it – this was what they'd come for.

The sirens grew louder.

Jack quickly grabbed a screenshot of the message, then scanned the rest of the emails. Seeing no others from Cloud, he pressed his eye back to the telescope. The fire had engulfed half the office. Slink still had a path clear to the window, but he had to be quick.

'Get out of there, Slink.'

Slink stepped to the window and reached for the hole, but his hand jerked.

He tried again but his whole arm shook and the gripper was randomly opening and closing.

'What are you doing?' Lux said. 'Hurry up.'

'I can't,' Slink said, breathless. 'This suit thing's gone nuts. I can't...control it.'

Jack heard a sharp intake of breath before Charlie said, 'It's my fault.'

'What do you mean?' Jack said, glancing between the buildings to his left as a fire engine came into view, its lights flashing.

'When I modified the exoskeleton,' Charlie continued, 'I didn't have time to seal all the wires. Water must be getting in.'

'Really great, Charlie.' Slink staggered back and almost fell over as he wrestled with the contraption.

'I wasn't expecting it to get wet,' Charlie said. 'I even checked the weather forecast. I'm sorry.'

'Is there any way to get it working again?' Lux said.

There was a short pause.

'No.'

Slink let out a huff of annoyance and started trying to free himself. It was a slow job because the exoskeleton was fighting him, making sharp, erratic movements.

Jack looked up and down the face of the building. There was no other way for Slink to escape. The only possible route was via a window cleaners' cradle, but he would still have to climb up to it. And that would be impossible without the exoskeleton because it was two storeys above him and the wind was far too strong – he'd be torn from the building.

Jack looked at Slink again – he'd now managed to free one arm and was wrestling with the straps on the other.

'Look, Jack.' Lux pointed.

At the base of the building, policemen and women were pouring out of the main entrance.

A fire engine pulled up and Jack could hear the distant siren of a second one on its way.

Several fire fighters jumped out, ran around the building and looked up at the smoke pouring from the hole in the window.

Jack refocused on the office. Slink was lying on the floor. He finally managed to wriggle out of the exoskeleton and jumped to his feet.

'Try the other door,' Jack said.

Holding his arm up, shielding his face from the fire, Slink hurried back to Chief Whitaker's office and over to the door to the corridor. 'It's locked.'

'Any way to break it down?'

'No.' Slink rushed to the open window again. 'I'm climbing.'

'No, Slink!' Lux said. 'You'll fall.'

'Wait.' Jack's eyes snapped up to the window cleaners' cradle. It was suspended under a swinging arm. 'Charlie, you see that platform above Slink?'

'Yes.'

'Any way to get it down to him?'

'Not that I can think of.'

Slink looked up. 'I'm going.'

Before Jack could stop him, Slink pulled himself out of the window and started to climb.

Jack glanced down – one of the firemen had spotted him and was now pointing.

Several firemen hurried into the building.

Slink made agonisingly slow progress and the next few minutes passed in anxious silence.

Jack glanced back at the laundry van and swung the telescope across the road. 'OK, Wren. There's nothing more you guys can do. Get out.'

The lights came back on in the shop.

Wren unlocked the door and looked down at the shopkeeper. 'I really am sorry.' She tossed a set of keys on to the floor, exited the shop, then hurried across the road and climbed into the laundry van.

The van drove off and disappeared around the corner.

Jack returned his attention to the police building.

Slink had managed to make it up to the next storey.

'Be careful, Slink,' Jack said.

'Aren't I always?'

'No, not so much.'

The wind tugged at his clothes, but somehow Slink managed to hold on. He hauled himself up a few extra centimetres, keeping his body as flat against the building as possible.

Jack winced. It wouldn't take much for Slink to fall. He could hardly bear to watch and turned the telescope towards the office window.

The door suddenly burst open and a funnel of water erupted into the room.

A minute later, the fire was out and firemen were moving through the office. One of them stepped cautiously to the window and peered out. Then he looked up and spotted Slink. He waved over one of his companions and they both looked up at him, confusion on their faces.

Slink glanced down and gave them a thumbs-up. 'All right?' he called.

One of the firemen held out his arms and beckoned Slink back to the window.

Slink shook his head. 'Nah, I'm OK here, mate.' He looked up at the cradle and continued to climb towards it.

The fireman pulled off his breather mask and shouted at him, but Slink ignored the guy and kept climbing.

Finally, Slink managed to grab hold of the bottom of the cradle and he hauled himself up.

Jack let out a huge breath.

Slink pressed a button on the cradle and it edged up the side of the building.

The fireman stared up at him, dumbfounded. Then he shouted again, pulled back and waved his arms about in frustration as he spoke with two of his colleagues.

When Slink reached the top, he leapt from the cradle and on to the roof.

'He's amazing,' Lux said in obvious awe.

'You need to be quick, Slink,' Jack said, looking back at the office as two of the firemen left the room. 'They're on their way up to you.'

Slink adjusted his hood and bandana, making sure his face was hidden from all the cameras on the roof.

Jack looked at the base of the building – police officers were gathered in small groups a safe distance away.

Had any of them spotted Slink too? Once the firemen told them about him, how long would it be before they locked down the building and started a search?

'Jack?'

He looked up.

Slink was standing by the exit door on the roof.

'Yeah?'

'If those men are on their way up here, where exactly do I go?'

Lux pulled the laptop close and concentrated on Slink's camera view. 'Slink, go through the exit,' she said.

'You sure?'

'Yes.' Lux glanced at Jack. 'Trust me.'

'OK.' Slink opened the door and entered the stair-well. He peered over the railing. 'I can hear them – they're two floors below and coming up,' he whispered.

'Get to the next level,' Lux said.

Slink hurried down the stairs, clearing four or five at a time. He reached the door to the next floor, threw it open and hurried inside.

'It's no good – I think they saw me. Which way do I go now?'

Lux took a deep breath and closed her eyes. She muttered under her breath before her eyes snapped open again. 'Third door on the right.'

Slink turned and sprinted down the hallway.

He opened the door she'd said, stepped inside and closed it behind him, just as the door to the stairwell banged open.

'He went this way,' a voice called.

'Turn around,' Lux whispered into her micro-phone. 'It's the door to your left.'

Slink went inside.

He was now standing in a bathroom.

Slink spun on the spot.

There were no doors or windows.

'Err, Lux?'

CHAPTER ELEVEN

THERE WAS A LOUD BANG.

Slink wheeled around and locked the bathroom door.

The handle rattled.

'Hey, kid, c'mon out of there.'

Jack looked at Lux. She had her eyes closed. 'What are you doing?'

Lux held up her hand – 'Trying to remember the layout of the building' – and squeezed her eyes tighter. 'OK.' She opened her eyes again. 'Slink. Air vent. Near the floor.'

Slink knelt down, grabbed the air vent grille and pulled it away from the wall. He then lay on his stomach and slithered into the opening head first.

Slink scrambled along on his belly until he reached a T-junction. 'Which way?' he whispered.

There was a cracking sound.

Obviously the firemen had broken into the bathroom.

'Hey, what are you doing?'

Slink looked back.

One of the men's faces peered into the air vent. He reached for Slink. 'Get out of there.'

'Lux?' Slink shouted, kicking out at the man's hands.

'Wait . . . left. Go left.'

Slink spun his body and twisted around the corner, away from the fireman.

He then crawled forward a few more metres until he reached another tunnel that went straight down.

Slink peered over the edge.

'That's a long drop,' he whispered. 'At least twenty metres.'

'Can you make it?' Jack said.

There was a short pause, then Slink said, 'Of course.'

He moved forward, managed to turn his body in the narrow space and started to lower himself down.

Jack glanced at Lux, and when he looked back at the screen again, Slink was already halfway to the bottom, bracing his feet either side and stepping down.

He stopped. 'Lux?'

'Yeah?'

'There's a huge fan.' He looked down.

Sure enough, directly below his feet was a set of spinning blades.

'It's OK,' Lux said. 'Keep going.'

'Are you sure?' Jack whispered to her.

She nodded, keeping her eyes on the laptop screen.

Slink hesitated a moment, then continued down.

When he was a metre from the fan, Lux said, 'Stop there.'

Slink stopped, and the noise from the fan drowned out his words.

'Turn to your right,' Lux said.

To Jack's relief, Slink could hear her and did as asked.

'OK,' Lux said. 'Shove the wall in front of you as hard as you can.'

Slink said something, but Jack couldn't make it out.

Slink then shifted his weight, put both of his hands on the metal wall in front of him and shoved.

Suddenly the wall gave way and Slink tumbled through the hole.

He landed on a lino floor, jumped to his feet and looked around.

He was in a small square room lined with shelves.

'Where am I?' he said.

'Maintenance room,' Lux said. 'That was an access panel to the air conditioning.'

Slink turned around, crept to the door and peered into the hallway. 'Empty,' he whispered.

'Go right,' Lux said. 'Exit door at the end.'

Slink followed her instructions, went through the door, down several flights of steps, along two more corridors and a narrow hallway and finally stopped at a carved wooden door.

'OK,' Lux said, taking a breath. 'On the other side of that is the main foyer.'

Slink opened the door a few centimetres and peered out.

There were five firemen and three police officers standing in a group, chatting and talking into their radios.

'Is there another way out?' Jack asked.

Lux shook her head. 'It's the only way.'

Without further hesitation, Slink slipped through the door and into the foyer.

With his back pressed against the wall, he silently edged his way towards the glass entrance door, not taking his eyes off the group.

One of the police officers turned and spoke into his radio. 'Say that again?'

Slink froze.

'He's gotta be up there somewhere. Try the next floor.' The cop turned back to the group.

Slink continued along the wall, reached the entrance and pushed it open.

He'd just stepped through when someone shouted, 'Hey!'

Slink turned and sprinted around the corner.

Two policemen ran after him, but Slink was way too fast for them. He vaulted a wall, ran across the road and vanished down an alleyway between two buildings.

Jack grinned at Lux. 'That was amazing.'

She smiled back at him. 'Thanks.'

They slid the telescope back into his bag, packed the laptop and silently moved from the edge of the roof.

• • •

Back at Serene's loft, everyone dropped into the chairs and sofas.

'That better have been worth all the hassle,' Charlie said.

Jack unzipped his bag and pulled out the laptop. 'It was.' He handed it to Charlie.

She unfolded it and her eyes scanned down the email. The further she got through it, the more confused she looked. But by the time she'd reached the end, she was smiling.

'What is it?' Wren said.

'It's an email to several other divisions within the NYPD and the Port Authority,' Jack said. 'Apparently our friend Chief Whitaker has told them all there's an FBI training exercise being carried out on North Brother Island.'

'But it's a bird sanctuary!' Lux said. 'It's off limits to the public anyway.'

'Yes,' Jack said, 'but the surrounding waterway isn't. It's regularly patrolled. The Chief has told the police and Port Authority to steer well clear of it.'

Lux nodded. 'And you think he's lying about the FBI training?'

'No doubt about it.' Jack looked between them all. 'North Brother Island must be where Hector is hiding.'

'Where is the island?' Wren asked.

'It's on the East River,' Drake said, leaning against the wall.

'Yeah,' Lux said. 'And it's full of abandoned buildings. There's nothing there.'

'Which makes it the perfect place for Hector to hide.' Jack frowned. 'We'll need to do a recon mission. Is there some way to take a look at the place?'

'No problem,' Drake said, striding to the spiral staircase. 'Give me a couple of hours.'

Jack gestured for Slink to follow him to the office. 'I've got a job for you too.'

• • •

After catching a bare twenty minutes of sleep, Jack, Charlie, Lux, Slink and Wren were standing on a wooden dock on the East River.

Jack heard a distant rumble of a boat's engine. He squinted into the darkness and could just make out its outline against the water.

He tensed. 'Wait.' As the boat came closer, he saw its markings. *Cops.*

Jack went to run, but Lux grabbed his arm. 'Relax,' she said. 'This is our ride.'

Jack stared at the police boat as it glided towards them, cutting a wave through the black water. 'Our ride?'

Lux smiled and nodded. 'Look.'

As the boat pulled alongside the dock, Jack could make out the driver – it was Drake.

'Nice boat,' Lux said to him, as if this were an everyday occurrence.

Drake idled the engine. 'Jump aboard.'

'Did he nick this?' Jack said into Lux's ear.

She shrugged. 'Borrowed.'

Jack thought that stealing a police boat was probably the dumbest thing anyone had ever done.

Charlie, Slink, Wren and Lux leapt on board.

Jack hesitated and thought about it a moment, but quickly came to the conclusion that they didn't have much choice. He glanced around, then followed the others.

'Next stop, North Brother Island.' Drake looked over his shoulder and reversed the boat along the dock, then turned and opened the throttle.

Charlie raised her voice above the roar of the engine. 'How long will it take us to get there?' she asked Drake.

'Twenty minutes.' He gestured to the police radio mounted in the dash. 'I'm listening out for them. I'll know if any of them are near.'

Jack sat next to Lux.

'What's the plan?' she said.

'Recon,' Jack said. 'Gather intelligence, then get back to the loft and plan a mission.'

'How many missions have you done?'

Jack stared at the lights on the shoreline as they sped past. 'Hundreds.'

• • •

Drake eased up on the throttle as North Brother Island loomed out of the darkness. It was crammed with trees.

Drake glanced back at the others. 'What do you want me to do?'

Jack got up and stood next to him. 'Can you just circle around it?'

Charlie unzipped her backpack and removed a military drone. It had four rotor blades and several tiny cameras. She switched it on. 'Obi?'

'I've got it,' Obi said in their ears. 'The signal's clear.'

Charlie held the drone above her head, the rotors fired up and it lifted into the air and disappeared over the island.

The next few minutes passed in eerie silence.

Drake kept his distance from the shoreline and the boat glided in a long arc.

As they circled, a large brick building several storeys high came into view. It was just visible among the trees, overgrown with vines.

To the right of the building were the remains of a pontoon, but there was no safe place to land the boat.

So far there was no sign of life – no lights, no movement, no other boats, nothing.

'Are you sure someone's here?' Drake said as they continued around the island.

'Hector's there all right,' Jack muttered under his breath.

He knew it.

A few more minutes passed as they continued their tour and occasionally they'd glimpse another ruined building among the trees.

Slink let out a huge breath. 'This. Is. Boring.'

Jack kept his eyes on the island and ignored him. He still couldn't see any signs of current human habitation.

Suddenly Obi said, 'Guys, it's found something.'

Jack glanced at Charlie. 'The drone?'

'Yeah. There's a camera mounted on the outside of one of those abandoned buildings. I've logged the position and now I'm sending the drone to search for more.'

Jack glanced at the others as if to say, *I told you so.*

A few minutes later and Obi spoke again. 'Drone has finished its sweep of the island. It's gathered basic point data. There are seven cameras and a few laser trips.'

'Any sign of where Hector is?' Jack said.

'No. The wires to all of the security features are well hidden. Can't see where they lead to and I don't want to risk sending the drone into any of the buildings. We might lose it.'

'OK,' Jack said. 'Do another sweep of the island, just in case there are any more cameras.'

'Will do.'

'What's point data?' Wren asked.

Jack turned to her. 'The drone has used a laser to measure and mark every building, tree, camera and laser trip on the island. It's so we can build a 3D map when we get back to the loft.'

Drake pointed at a small beach as it came into view. 'Want me to land there, Jack?'

'No. Please keep going.'

'Wait,' Slink said, exasperated. 'Come on, Jack. Let me go check it out. It's no use just sitting here.

Every minute we waste is another minute Hector could be setting up hackers and stealing secret documents.'

Jack hesitated. 'OK,' he said finally. 'But remember what we discussed and be careful – don't disturb anything.' Last thing Jack wanted on his conscience was the destruction of some rare bird nesting site.

'I'll be as stealthy as a ninja on a cloud,' Slink said, rubbing his hands together. 'Or not.' He winked.

Jack nodded at Drake.

Drake eased back on the throttle and aimed the boat at the shoreline. When he was a few metres out, he cut the engine entirely and the boat's nose kissed the shore.

Slink leapt off the bow, glanced around, then followed a path into the trees and vanished.

There was a buzzing sound.

The drone flew over the boat and Charlie caught it.

'Sweep of the island is complete,' Obi said. 'Can't see any more cameras and I've gathered as much point data as I can.'

Charlie returned the drone to her bag and everyone waited in silence.

As the minutes passed, Jack's stomach tightened.

He wasn't sure this was going to plan.

Suddenly there was a light through the trees.

'What's Slink up to?' Charlie said. 'He should know better than to use his torch.'

Drake hurried to the bow of the boat and shoved it off the beach with his foot.

'What are you doing?' Charlie hissed.

Drake climbed back in front of the wheel and went to start the engine.

'No!' Wren said, grabbing his arm. 'We're not leaving Slink behind.'

'Now we're ready to go when he arrives,' Drake said.

'Guys?' Lux pointed.

Wren and Charlie gasped as several figures emerged, striding down the path Slink had taken.

As they came closer, Jack recognised their out-lines – Connor, and the hulking frame of Monday. Monday had Slink by the shoulders.

Hector was in the lead and Jack could just make out the self-satisfied smirk on his face.

Hector opened his arms wide. 'Jack, it's so nice to see you here.' His gaze moved over Lux and Drake. 'New recruits for your merry band of vagrants?'

'Give him back,' Jack said.

Hector glanced at Slink. 'I don't think so. Not this time.' His eyes locked on to Wren for a moment, then moved to Jack again. 'I have no idea how you found me, or how you got here, but your friend will be our insurance. If you come near this island again, I will kill him.'

Slink struggled, but winced when Monday's grip tightened on his shoulder.

'Well?' Hector cocked his head. 'What are you waiting for?' He waved them off. 'Go away.'

Jack looked at Drake and nodded.

Drake started the engine.

'No...' Wren said, rushing forward.

Jack held her back. 'There's nothing we can do.'

Hector remained frozen, staring at them, as the boat backed away. Even though it was dark, Jack could still make out the hatred in Del Sarto's eyes. The man wanted to kill them all, and Jack had a feeling that he already had a plan for how to do that.

Drake put the boat into forward gear and they moved from the island.

Jack sat on the bench and glanced over his shoulder.

Hector and his cronies were marching Slink back through the trees, towards one of the buildings.

'They must have seen him on one of their cameras,' Lux said.

Jack nodded. 'Yeah, that's what I expected.'

The others frowned at him.

'You what?' Charlie said. 'Wait a minute, if you expected –'

Jack held up a hand and spoke into his headset. 'How are you doing, Obi?'

'I've got a clear signal, and I'm recording it like you said.'

Wren crossed her arms. 'What signal?'

Jack looked at each of them in turn. 'I thought there was a good chance Hector would have the island well protected. So Slink volunteered to get caught.'

Charlie stared at him. 'He got caught on purpose?'

Jack nodded.

'Why?'

'Well, I couldn't see any other way for us to do a proper recon mission. The drone was good, but it needed someone on the ground to scope the place out. Someone to get us eyes inside the buildings.'

'Ah,' Lux said, smiling. 'I get it – Slink's wearing a camera, isn't he?'

Jack nodded again. 'And a mic.'

Wren looked furious. She balled her fists. 'Why didn't you tell us?'

Jack spoke in a calm voice. 'If we all knew it was a trick, Hector would've been able to tell. I couldn't risk that. I needed it to be believable. He had to be convinced he'd captured Slink himself.'

Wren's face screwed up and her cheeks flushed. 'I'm the best actor out of all of us. I've tricked loads of –'

'I know,' Jack said. 'But you care about Slink too much, and Hector knows that too. That's why he looked straight at you. Remember?'

Wren huffed and turned away.

'I'm sorry, Wren. I did what I thought was best.' Jack glanced at Drake. 'Can this boat go any faster?'

A smile swept across Drake's face. 'Hold on to your hats.' He opened the throttle and the bow of the boat rose into the air by several feet, then crashed back to the surface of the water and they sped into the darkness.

• • •

Jack hurried straight into Serene's office, with Charlie, Lux, Drake and Wren following close behind. They all gathered around Obi at the computer.

On the screen in front of him was a darkened image of a doorway. Torchlight glinted off the lens of a camera in the corner of the wall and ceiling.

Obi was making a note of where the camera was located. 'Hector's well paranoid,' he said. 'He's set up loads of cameras.'

'Is that from Slink's hidden camera?' Wren asked.

Obi nodded.

'Where are they?' Jack said.

Obi sped the recording back until the image was outside again. As they walked, with Hector in the lead, they followed a broken path through the trees, picking their way carefully over debris and rubble from the abandoned buildings.

After a while, they pushed through an overgrown bush and a large brick structure loomed before them.

'That's the main building – the first one we saw,' Charlie said.

Jack leant in to the screen and watched closely.

As Hector walked through a door, Jack saw the first sign of technology – the high-resolution camera mounted above the frame.

They marched down a corridor with several more cameras and motion sensors, then entered a vast room.

Most of the paint had peeled from the walls, and large chunks of concrete and plaster had fallen from the ceiling. A thick layer of dust coated the floor.

The room looked as though it might once have been a hospital ward, because there were rusty metal beds and chairs piled up against the far wall.

The middle of the room was different – it had been swept clean and there was a glass box, hexagonal in shape, about four metres on each side and three metres tall.

The group strode over to the box. Hector entered a code on a keypad, opened a door and went inside.

Monday grabbed Slink and shoved him through, closing the door behind them. Then he forced Slink to sit in a chair in one corner and tied him to it with rope.

Connor, Cloud and Monday then sat in their own chairs, each facing a different direction.

Slink's view panned slowly around the glass room.

Against one of the far walls was a metal rack holding row upon row of circuit boards, all with red and blue lights blinking.

'What's all that?' Drake said.

'A custom computer he's built.' Charlie leant in to get a better look too.

Jack frowned. Each circuit board was connected by hundreds of wires, and there was a stack of hard drives at one end of the rack. That, no doubt, was where Hector would store the stolen data he collected.

Jack wondered how many top-secret documents Hector had managed to acquire so far. How many secrets had he pinched?

At the end of the rack was a junction box with several cables going out through the wall, snaking across the floor and disappearing under a door.

Next to the junction box were two black cylinders, one and a half metres high by half a metre wide.

'What are they?' Jack said, as the camera lingered on them.

Charlie's eyes narrowed. 'Not sure.'

There was another thick cable that ran from the main computer stack and went straight up through the ceiling.

Jack pointed at it. 'What about that?'

'If I had to guess,' Charlie said, 'I would say it was a communications feed.'

'It is.' Obi brought up one of the images from the drone.

On the roof of the building was a large satellite dish.

'Hector must have good tech support,' Lux said. 'That's clever.'

'Knowing Hector,' Obi said, 'it's probably hooked up to his own private satellite or something.' He clicked the image and returned to Slink's camera view of inside the glass box.

In the middle of the room was a desk with several monitors, a few keyboards and a chair.

Hector was sitting in the chair. He glanced over at Slink, then flexed his fingers and started to type. After a minute he looked up again. 'It seems as if your friends took my advice and got out of here.'

'Great,' Slink said. 'You can let me go then.'

A cruel smile played on Hector's lips. 'I'm going to keep you here for a while yet. I have to pay you Urban Outlaw brats back for all the trouble you've caused me and my father.'

'Oh, yeah,' Slink said, with a heavy measure of sarcasm in his voice. 'How is your dad? Still a bit burnt around the edges?'

Hector's face twisted with rage and he balled his fists. 'He's still in a coma, thanks to you.'

'No,' Slink said. 'That was *his* fault.'

Hector stared at Slink for a while, then seemed to relax. 'I'm going to burn *you*. Everything my father felt, I'll return a thousand times.'

Wren grabbed Jack's arm.

'That won't happen,' Jack said. Though he didn't feel as sure as he sounded.

After a moment, Hector's focus moved back to the screens in front of him and he started typing again.

The view from Slink's camera continued to pan around the room. Occasionally it would stop on a heat sensor or computer terminal long enough for the camera to focus and send a clear image.

Finally, with the sweep of the room complete, Slink's view centred back on Hector.

Jack straightened up and looked at Charlie. 'Well?'

She shook her head. 'It looks impossible.'

'Exactly what I was thinking.'

CHAPTER TWELVE

OBI TURNED IN HIS CHAIR TO LOOK AT JACK AND Charlie. 'Are you two serious? Why's it impossible to break into Hector's hideout?'

'Yeah, right,' Wren said. 'Why's it so hard?'

Jack pointed at the screen. 'First, that box they're in.'

Wren frowned.

'It's made of glass, so Hector and his henchmen have three-hundred and sixty degrees of visibility. They'll spot anyone coming. That's if anyone actually gets past the rest of their security.' Jack reached over, took the mouse and sped the recording back to where Slink was entering the main room. 'Look at this.' There were several lights mounted to floor-standing poles in each corner of the room. Some were pointed at the centre, while others lit up the rest of the space around it. He let the recording move forward frame by frame as Slink walked. 'There are tamper-proof cameras inside the glass room and all around the outside. 'Speaking of which' – he turned to Obi – 'how many cameras did the drone find?'

'Fourteen.'

Jack sighed. 'That's how he knew we were there and when we'd left. Not to mention all the motion and heat sensors he's got set up too. There's no way we're getting near that island without him knowing about it.'

Everyone stood in silence for a long while, staring at the monitor.

Wren muttered something under her breath.

Charlie glanced at her. 'What?'

'I said,' Wren looked at Jack, 'why didn't Hector just kill us when he had the chance?'

Jack stared at her for a moment, then his eyes widened. 'She's right.'

'He couldn't,' Charlie said. 'The gunshots would have drawn too much attention.'

'Yes,' Jack said, pacing back and forth, thinking, 'but there's another reason too.'

'What do you mean?' Lux said.

'Hector could have put a gun to Slink's head, demanded we all get off the boat, then taken us to one of those derelict buildings and killed us there.'

'OK,' Charlie said. 'So why didn't he?'

Jack stopped pacing and looked at them all. 'He wants us to break in.'

Wren's eyebrows knitted together. 'He what?'

'Think about it,' Jack said, resuming his pacing. 'Even if Hector and his gang had killed us in some abandoned building on that island, eventually someone would have found the bodies, right?'

Lux nodded. 'It's a bird sanctuary. Conservationists go there now and again to check the nests.'

'So what?' Obi said. 'It's New York. Don't people get shot here all the time?'

Drake laughed.

'Maybe not *all* the time, Obi,' Lux said with a smile.

Obi's cheeks reddened. 'Sorry.'

Jack turned to Lux. 'If the police here found the bodies of six teenagers, all murdered, what would happen?'

'It would be national news.'

'Manhunt?'

'Yeah, and the rest,' Drake said. 'They wouldn't stop until they caught the people responsible.'

'And who told the police to stay away from the island in the first place?'

'Chief Whitaker,' Wren said.

'Exactly,' Jack said. 'He has emails linking himself to Hector. He'd be in serious trouble.'

'I'm confused,' Wren said. 'Does all of this mean that Hector can't kill Slink or any of us?'

Charlie gasped. 'No.' She looked at Jack. 'I get what you're saying.'

'What's he saying?' Wren sounded impatient.

Charlie swallowed, glanced at the monitor, then looked back at the others again. 'Jack's saying that Hector wants us dead, right?'

They all nodded.

Charlie continued, 'But he can't just murder us. It would draw way too much attention.'

'So?' Wren said.

'So,' Jack said, 'he'll want to make our deaths look like an accident.' He gestured to the screen. 'He wants us to try and break Slink out of there and then, *oops*.'

Lux's eyes widened at that. 'He's set a trap?'

'Yes,' Jack said. 'Hector hoped we'd follow him over here and he's planned for the eventuality that we'd catch up with him.' He glanced at the screen, then at the others. 'By going there, we'd be playing straight into his hands.'

Obi waved a finger at the screen. 'He must know that Slink is wearing a camera too.'

'Yep.' Jack watched the screen as Hector continued to type and click. Who was he setting up now? What was he hacking into? What was his overall plan? Jack let out a long breath. Getting Slink out of there was likely to be the most difficult mission they'd ever attempted, and there wasn't any room for error.

● ● ●

Thirty minutes later, Jack was still sitting in front of the monitor in Serene's office. He'd watched Slink's recording over and over, soaking up every detail of the island, the main building and the glass room.

'Hey.' Charlie walked into the office, pulled up a chair and sat next to him. 'Any luck?'

Jack shook his head. 'I can't see where the trap is, but I'm not surprised by that.'

'Can you guess where it is?'

'Yeah, I think so.'

Charlie nodded at the screen. 'Want to show me?'

'Well, Hector would think that we'd plan this like any other mission, right? That we would look for a weakness, concentrate on that, break in and try to destroy the virus.'

'OK,' Charlie said. 'Sounds reasonable.'

'He's made sure the security is tight.'

'To make it look convincing?'

'Exactly,' Jack said. 'But more importantly, he's left one tiny weakness, to steer us in that direction.'

'What weakness?'

Jack brought up a screen grab of the end of the racks with the circuit boards. He pointed at the power breaker on the wall. 'One of the cables leaves through that.' His finger traced the path of a wire as it left the room, meandered across the floor and disappeared through a doorway.

'You think there's a power generator in there, don't you?' Charlie said.

'Yes. And I've also worked out that the room has an external wall, which means –'

'It's probably got a window.'

Jack nodded. 'Hector expects us to break into that room, destroy the generator and shut down all his security.'

'OK,' Charlie said. 'But if that's true, how would that get *all* of us killed? It would take only one person to get in there and shut off the generator.'

'I'm not sure. My guess is there's some sort of trap that would need all of us to get past it. Something that means we'd all have to be in there at the same time. Or, maybe, one of us would get trapped and the others would come to the rescue. I don't know, and we have no way to find out.'

Charlie looked thoughtful. 'Have you seen another way in?'

'Not yet.'

She leant into the display for a moment, examining Hector's computer set-up. Finally she straightened up. 'That generator room can't be the main source of power.'

'I know,' Jack said. 'I thought the same thing – there's no way Hector would even let us anywhere near the generator, but I can't see another way for him to power all of that stuff.' He brought up a screenshot he'd taken from Slink's camera earlier. It showed another thick cable, which rose from the end of the rack, went up through the glass roof and on into the ceiling of the room above. 'I tried looking at that to see if we could at least cut Hector off from the outside world. It's the only way he can connect to the internet.'

'And?' Charlie said. 'Let me guess – he's got that well protected?'

'Yeah.' Jack sighed, sat back in his chair and they both stared at the screen.

'Wait a minute.' Charlie sat forward again. 'Is there a better view of those?' She pointed at the two black cylinders next to the junction box.

Jack rewound the recording to the moment Hector walked into the glass cube. As soon as he opened the door, Jack froze the image.

Charlie leant in till her nose was inches away from the screen.

Finally she sat back and grinned.

Jack looked at her. 'What is it?'

'Hector's mistake.' She pointed at the two cylinders. 'I think I know what those are. Can you get a layout of the building somehow?'

'Already tried.' Obi came waddling into the office, stuffing his face with some kind of small rectangular cakes.

Charlie grimaced. 'What are those, Obi?'

He shrugged. 'A sponge thing. It has cream inside.'

'I can tell,' Charlie said. 'It's all around your face.'

Obi wiped his mouth with the back of his sleeve and held one out to her. 'They're good.'

Charlie shook her head. 'Nah, you're all right. I'll grab something later.'

'What were you just saying?' Jack asked Obi.

'Huh?'

Jack gestured to the screen. 'About getting a plan of the building.'

'Oh, yeah, right.' Obi sat down in a spare chair. 'I looked while you lot were on your way back here, and I couldn't find anything.'

Charlie glanced at the screen, then at Jack. 'I need a layout of the place. If I can get that, I reckon we'd have a good chance of beating Hector at his own game.' She explained her idea to them.

When she was finished, Jack stared at the screen, thinking. Now he understood why she needed a plan of the building. All he had to do was get Charlie inside, and she could do the rest. Only thing was, that was going to be difficult to achieve.

'Wait a minute, I have a crazy idea,' Jack said, finally tearing his gaze from the screen. He explained what he had in mind. 'Go speak to Lux and Drake. See if they can help you gather the materials we need.'

Charlie stood up and walked to the door.

'Charlie?'

She turned back.

'Also, ask Drake if he can keep that boat a little longer. But if there's a chance he might get caught, see if he can get another one somehow.'

'OK.' Charlie left the office.

Jack turned to Obi. 'We need every picture you can find on the internet of North Brother Island and all its buildings. Gather as much metadata as you can too.'

Obi slid his chair in front of the computer, flexed his fingers and started the search.

Jack marched over to the dining table, scooped up a bag from the floor and pulled out the laptop. He brought up a command box on the screen and started typing.

After a few minutes Wren came over. 'Sorry.'

Jack looked at her. 'For what? It's me who should be sorry. I should've told you what Slink was going to do.'

'Nah,' Wren said, half smiling. 'Probably best I didn't know.' She nodded at the display. 'What are you doing?'

'Downloading a program from the bunker's computers.' Jack pulled out the chair next to him. 'You can watch if you like.'

Wren sat down.

Jack glanced over at the gadget room – Charlie was talking to Lux and Drake, while examining the equipment on the shelves.

'Do you fancy her?' Wren said.

'Huh?' Jack broke his gaze. 'Who?'

Wren cocked her head to the side and gave him a cheeky smile. 'Lux, of course.'

Jack focused on the laptop screen. 'No.'

Wren snorted. 'Yeah, right.'

Jack let out an annoyed breath. 'Just watch this.'

When the program from the bunker's computers had finished downloading, he opened it. Code scrolled down the screen. Jack checked it, made the necessary adjustments so it fitted its new purpose and ran the program.

A three-dimensional, wire-frame cube appeared on the screen.

Jack accessed Serene's network and transferred the point data and camera positions Obi had gathered from the drone to the program.

Just as he finished, Obi sent the images of North Brother Island he'd downloaded from the internet.

When Jack was all done, he said, 'Watch this.' And clicked the Run button.

The program started to work its magic – hundreds of images flashed up, angled themselves, then dissolved into the three-dimensional cube.

'What's it doing?' Wren said.

'Combining all the data. The images, camera positions, GPS coordinates...' Jack stood, strode to the gadget room and went inside.

Drake was gathering equipment from a list and loading it into bags.

Charlie and Lux were sitting at the workbench. Charlie was concentrating on the laptop that was connected to the 3D printer.

Next to her were hundreds of pieces of Serene's gadgets that she'd dismantled and robbed for parts.

'She's not going to thank you for that,' Jack said.

'Huh?' Charlie looked up at him and followed his gaze. 'Oh, right, yeah.' She reached over the worktop and picked up a metal cylinder. 'We need to wedge this in Hector's computer.' She then brought up a picture of the computer in the glass hexagon. She zoomed in on a point between two circuit boards. 'Jam this cylinder in there. OK?'

Jack shrugged. 'Sure. What does it do?'

'It's basically a cluster of capacitors and batteries.' She handed Jack a key fob. 'When you press that button, the cylinder will release thousands of volts, destroying the computer components.'

'Right,' Jack said. 'But we can't just destroy it.' He glanced at Lux. 'We need to get evidence that Hector's been setting people up.'

'Already thought of that,' Charlie said. She reached up to a shelf and grabbed a black cube, three centimetres on each side. She turned it so Jack could see it had network connectors on each face. 'Plug this into the port. It'll connect to Serene's servers here. Obi will then need a few minutes to locate the evidence and download it. After that, we're free to destroy the computer – including Hector's hacking program – and get out.'

'Brilliant,' Jack said. 'Now I've got to work out how to get us inside Hector's lair.'

'How's the layout of the island going?' Lux asked.

'That's why I'm here,' Jack said. 'It'll be done in a minute or so. Want to see it?'

Lux jumped off her stool. 'Please.'

Charlie rolled her eyes behind Lux's back and stood up.

At the dining table, Charlie, Obi, Lux and Wren gathered around Jack.

He looked at the image count – one hundred and thirty to go. 'It's almost done.'

The images flashed up on the screen one after another in rapid succession and the counter logged them.

Finally a blue message scrolled across the screen:

COMPOSITION COMPLETE.

Jack hit another button and a three-dimensional view of the island appeared within the wire-frame cube. He moved his finger over the mouse pad and used the arrow keys to zoom in.

All the images Obi had downloaded were now in various positions, some lined up with one another, some overlapping. There were large gaps between them, and a few looked as if they were in the wrong position, but the overall effect was better than Jack could have hoped for.

Now they had a three-dimensional model of the island, complete with camera positions and angles.

'That's really clever,' Lux said.

Jack took a breath. 'Now for the moment of truth.' He steered the view towards the main building, over to the door which Hector had marched Slink through.

He eased forward, through the door and down the corridor. Finally he reached the main room and swung inside.

There were only a few images in here, and they were more crudely aligned, but it was enough to get a good sense of the room.

Jack then moved the camera view to the back wall and turned it to the left.

There was a door.

'That's the generator room,' Charlie said, pointing at the ghosted outline of the cables on the floor. 'That's where Hector expects us to break in.'

Jack moved through the door.

Beyond was a small room. It was dark, but high on the wall was a narrow, broken window. 'And that's where he wants us to get in.'

It was weird, looking at pictures people had taken of the room months or even years before, knowing that it now held some sort of trap.

In the images the room was empty, perhaps an old store cupboard. What had Hector put in there? Metal traps? A bomb of some kind?

'How are we going to get up to that window?' Wren said, looking at it. 'We need Slink.'

'Not sure yet.' Jack steered the view back to the main room.

Charlie pointed at the ghosted outlines of the computers, chairs and desk. 'Here.' She indicated the two cylinders. 'Can you look behind the wall here, Jack?'

He moved the camera view past the cylinders and glided through the right-hand wall.

On the other side was another room. There was only one grainy image of it, but it was enough to pick up the details they needed. This room had only one door and no windows.

'That's our target,' Charlie said, looking excited. 'That room.'

Jack nodded, understanding what she was getting at, and indicated the door at the other end. 'I bet Hector has that either blocked or protected.' He swung the view up to the top corner of the photo and could just make out a hole in the ceiling. Concrete had fallen into the room, exposing floor beams from the one above. 'That's our way in.'

'So,' Charlie said, 'we have a target, but how are we going to get to it?'

Jack pondered this a moment. 'We'll need to make sure we follow exact paths once we get to North Brother Island.'

'That won't be easy,' Lux said.

'I have an idea,' Obi said to Jack. 'Can you mark a route on the three-dimensional plan?'

Jack nodded. 'Sure. But how does that help us?'

Obi looked at Charlie. 'You can link it in with Serene's AR Glasses?'

They were one of Serene's high-tech gadgets. They consisted of a small headband mounted with a camera, a screen over one eye, microphone and earpiece, and inside was a small computer – the ultimate in augmented reality and communication.

Charlie hesitated, then smiled. 'Of course. We can overlay the digital images on the real world.'

'That's brilliant, Obi,' Lux said.

Obi glanced at her and his cheeks flushed.

Jack stood up. 'Drake?'

Drake walked into the room. 'What's up?'

'Any idea what Slink did with those inflatable people he got from the studio?'

'Yeah,' Drake said, smiling. 'Why?'

CHAPTER THIRTEEN

AN HOUR LATER, JACK, CHARLIE, OBI, WREN, Lux and Drake were on the police boat, heading towards North Brother Island.

When they were a mile or so out, Drake idled the engine, stepped away from the wheel and turned around to face the others. 'Are you sure this will work?' He looked at Jack.

'It'll be fine.' Jack glanced between Drake, Lux and Wren. 'Are you all clear on the mission?'

They nodded.

'OK,' Charlie said. 'Let's do it.' She reached into her bag and pulled out four masks that she'd made using Serene's 3D printer.

Jack took one of them and stared down at it. It was an exact duplicate of Drake's face.

Wren shuddered. 'That's creepy.'

'Understatement,' Obi said.

Jack nodded. Wren was right – it was creepy, especially with the real Drake standing right there. The detail was fantastic – all the way down to a mole on his cheek.

Lux took a mask of Charlie, and Charlie had Lux's.

Drake grabbed the final mask – of Jack.

Jack looked at Charlie. 'You got those other two?' he asked. She nodded.

The four of them glanced at each other a moment, then put on their masks and lifted their hoods to hide the edges.

To Jack, it was the weirdest feeling in the world – he was staring back at his own face. He let out a puff of air. 'Remember to turn your face to the light as you pass the cameras,' he said. 'Let Hector get a good look.'

'Not too good,' Charlie said. 'We don't want to push our luck.'

'Why don't I get a mask?' Obi said.

Wren rolled her eyes. 'We need to look like us, remember?'

Obi shrugged and picked up a backpack. 'I quite like the idea of being someone else now and again.'

'You know what to do?' Drake said to Jack, indicating the helm of the boat.

'I think so,' Jack said.

'Push on the throttle to go forward, back to reverse and the middle is neutral.' Drake smiled. 'Push harder to go faster. That big circular thing – just turn it in the direction you want to go.'

Wren giggled.

'Well, err, Drake,' Drake said in a mock British accent. 'Please take us to North Brother Island.'

Jack stepped to the helm. He gently pushed forward on the throttle and aimed the bow of the boat around the island.

Charlie stood beside him. 'I don't get it.'

'Don't get what.'

Charlie adjusted her mask. 'There's no way Hector won't see through this.'

'I know,' Jack said, keeping his focus on the water ahead. 'I expect Hector to realise these are masks. In fact, I'm banking on it for the mission to work.'

The last time they'd seen Hector in London was at the top of the Shard. They'd used a friend of theirs called Raze to stand in Slink's place. Hector had fallen for it that time, but Jack was fully aware he'd be on the lookout for tricks like that now.

Charlie turned to him. 'I don't understand.'

'No time to explain.' Jack nodded at the island as they rounded the corner.

A small beach loomed in the darkness. Jack eased back on the throttle and they glided to the shore. Obi, Drake, Lux and Wren stepped forward.

As soon as the bow touched the sand, Drake jumped from the boat and helped the other three on to the island.

'Remember to follow the exact path we planned,' Jack said. 'Don't deviate. Any problems, let us know straight away.'

'What happens if Hector comes out?' Wren said.

'He won't,' Jack said. 'He wants us to go to him.'

Drake nodded and pushed the boat back into deeper water.

Jack put it in reverse and moved away from the island.

Lux gave a small wave as they hurried up the path between the trees.

After a few minutes Obi said, 'I'm in position and patched in to Hector's cameras. I can see everything he can. I'll send the signal to you.'

'OK.' Jack glanced at Charlie, then opened the throttle and headed around to the other side of the island.

When they reached it, Jack slowed the boat and looked at the display on the laptop Charlie placed in front of him. The screen was now divided into sixteen separate boxes, each showing a different view of the island, some inside and some out.

Charlie pointed at the image showing Hector, Connor, Cloud, Monday and Slink. They were all still sitting inside the glass box.

Hector's gaze was fixed on one of the screens in front of him.

'You were right,' Charlie said. 'He hasn't ordered any of them to intercept us.' She pulled two pairs of the AR Glasses from her bag. 'Here.'

Jack fitted one on over the mask of Drake's face.

Charlie put on her own pair as Jack reached over to the laptop and typed a few commands. A three-dimensional view of the island appeared on the screen.

'Calibrating augmented reality,' he said. 'Look at the island.'

Both of them turned their heads and the image in the devices' screens swung around and zoomed in and out until it lined up perfectly with the real world.

Now Jack and Charlie could see the island in three dimensions, along with the photographs Obi had collected, all overlaid in front of them. The virtual outlines were in blues and greens, with a green arrow showing their planned route.

Jack followed it and glided the boat alongside a ramshackle pontoon that jutted out.

Charlie hopped off and tied the bowline to part of the rotten structure.

Jack switched off the boat's engine and carefully climbed out after her. He reached into the boat, handed Charlie a long cylinder with a strap and grabbed a duffel bag.

As they picked their way over the decaying timbers, Jack whispered into his headset, 'Obi?'

'Yeah?'

'We're calibrated. Patch us in to the others.'

'OK.'

The screen image flickered, and in the bottom corner was another small window. It showed a view from Lux's camera.

She was hurrying after Drake and Wren. They were jogging along the wall of the main building, pretending to keep out of sight of the CCTV cameras. But Jack knew Hector would have a clear view of them and hopefully their faces too. He'd focus most of his attention on them, thinking they were the real Urban Outlaws, while Jack and Charlie, disguised as Drake and Lux, would have a little more freedom to move about.

'Come on,' Jack whispered to Charlie, and they picked their way carefully along the pontoon. When they'd made it safely ashore, Jack stopped.

Ahead he could see the blue and green lines representing the data the drone had captured. A golden cone-shaped beam extended across a gap in the trees ahead.

Jack turned his head and his gaze followed the aim of the beam until it stopped at a camera mounted high on the wall of an abandoned building.

Jack glanced at Charlie. 'Ready?'

She adjusted her mask and nodded.

The two of them walked along a broken path and stepped into view of the camera, making sure it got a brief look at their faces.

Charlie set down her bag just out of the camera's range and opened it. Next she pulled out a small air pump attached to a high-capacity battery.

Jack took out two bundles of clothes from the duffel bag and set them on the ground next to her.

Charlie connected the hose from the air pump to a valve that stuck out of the clothes.

She pressed the button on the air pump and it started up.

Jack spoke quietly into the headset. 'Obi?'

'As far as I can tell, Hector is still watching the others.'

Jack stood and moved in front of the nearest camera's view again. He paced back and forth, glancing at his watch, as if waiting for the Outlaws.

'How are they getting on?' he whispered.

'I'll patch you in.'

The image in the corner of Jack's vision changed to the view from one of Hector's cameras.

Drake, Lux and Wren were crouched down by the wall of the main building. Above their heads was the small window to the power room.

Drake was taking his time, tying knots into a rope with a hook on the end.

So far everything was going to plan. Drake, Lux and Wren would never have to climb through that window. All they needed to do was stall for long enough so that Jack and Charlie could set everything up.

Jack turned back.

Charlie had inflated one set of clothes and was just finishing with the second.

She looked up at him and smiled.

There were now two dummies. All they needed were the finishing touches.

Charlie reached into her jacket and pulled out another two masks. Another Lux and another Drake. She put the Lux mask on a dummy and topped it with a pair of fake AR glasses. Then she carried the dummy to the edge of the camera's field of view, just out of sight.

Jack walked under the camera, as if he was still pacing back and forth, waiting. 'OK, Obi,' he whispered.

Obi brought up an image of the camera next to them. 'Ready, Charlie.'

Charlie eased the dummy of Lux forward a centimetre at a time until it just showed at the edge of the camera's view.

'Right,' Obi said. 'That's enough.'

Charlie tied the wrist of the dummy to a tree trunk, then carefully stepped back.

Jack smiled. From Hector's screen, it would look as if Lux was standing there.

'Now you,' Charlie whispered.

She scooped up the second dummy and hurried around to the other side of the camera as Jack casually walked out of its view.

Charlie fixed the second Drake mask and glasses under the dummy's hood and passed it to him.

Jack walked back to the camera. 'Tell me when, Obi.' He edged forward.

'Wait.' Charlie disappeared into the darkness and returned a minute later, carrying a heavy log. She dropped it at Jack's feet and took the dummy from him. 'It will look odd if they're both standing still.'

Jack understood.

He rolled the log with his foot and nudged it into the camera's field of view. Then he stepped back and held his breath. 'Obi?'

'Hector hasn't moved.'

Jack turned around.

Charlie had used string to tie the dummy into a sitting position.

'We need a distraction,' Jack said. 'It's too obvious.'

'On it,' Wren said.

The image in the corner of the AR Glasses showed Wren slipping off her backpack and removing some kind of device. She switched it on, LEDs blinked and she waved it over the building's wall, as if scanning for something.

'Well done, Wren. It's working,' Obi said. 'Hector's leaning in to his screen and he looks well confused.'

'Quick,' Jack said to Charlie.

They each took an arm of the dummy, sat him on the log in front of the camera and pulled back again.

'Well?' Jack asked.

There was a short pause, then Obi said, 'All good. Hector still seems to be distracted.'

Jack looked at the image of Wren. She was waving the device over the wall. 'What is that?'

Wren held it up as if checking a readout. 'It's that game Serene gave me – Hamster Escape.' After a moment more, she slipped it back into her bag.

Jack smiled. 'That was clever.'

'Thanks.'

He looked at the dummies in front of the camera, then at Charlie. 'We have to be quick.'

She nodded and, now they were free to move on, Jack and Charlie circled the camera, keeping out of its vision, and picked their way between the trees.

They followed the green arrow on the AR Glasses until they reached a clearing.

Ahead was another camera, the glasses' golden cone shape showing its field of view.

'I hope the drone mapped this accurately,' Jack whispered to Charlie.

An error of even a few centimetres might lead to Hector spotting them. Jack took a deep breath and he and Charlie followed the green arrow around the edge of the clearing.

Finally they made it to the end wall of the main building.

Above them, on the first floor, was a small window. By the looks of it, its glass and frame had fallen out a long time ago.

Jack looked at the image of Drake, Lux and Wren in his AR Glasses. Drake had finished tying knots into the rope and was now swinging the grappling hook on its end back and forth, ready to try to grip the window above.

He couldn't keep on stalling for ever – Jack and Charlie had to get a move on. Jack looked up at their target window. Now they were there, it looked higher than he'd expected. He glanced at her. 'Can you make it?'

As if in answer, Charlie stepped forward, gripped the brickwork and started to climb.

Jack watched for several anxious minutes as Charlie made her way up the wall of the building.

Soon she reached the window ledge and peered down at him as if to say, *Who needs Slink?*

Jack nodded. 'Nice one.'

Charlie lowered a rope, which Jack fixed to his harness and started to climb.

He was surprised how quickly he got tired.

By the time he hauled himself over the window frame, he was out of breath and his arms were burning. Suddenly he had a newfound respect for Slink's skills. He made it look so effortless.

Jack untied the rope, slipped it into his backpack and turned around. They were standing in a hallway. The floorboards were broken and in an advanced state of decay.

The green arrow on the AR Glasses pointed straight ahead.

Jack signalled Charlie to follow him and to watch her step.

Staying close to the wall, they made their way slowly up the corridor until they reached a door on the right. The green arrow was telling them to go inside.

Jack glanced back at Charlie, then opened the door and stepped into the room.

The space beyond was only a few metres on each side and almost the entire centre of the floor was missing.

In the room below was a power generator, its motor chugging. Charlie had been right – there was a cage surrounding the generator and a security camera pointed at it. If either of them tried to get near it, Hector would know. But, if Charlie's plan worked, they wouldn't have to.

Jack knelt down by the hole and pulled out the coil of rope from his backpack. He clipped one end to the harness under his clothes then lay on the floor.

Charlie sat on the edge of the hole and clipped the other end of the rope to her own harness. With care, Jack lowered her down just beyond the camera's view.

After a minute Charlie's feet touched the floor below. She looked up at Jack and gave him the signal that she was OK.

Jack unclipped the rope, stood up and took several deep breaths, preparing himself for the next part of the mission.

Finally ready, he left the room, but instead of climbing back through the window he went to the other end of the hallway and down a flight of stairs.

At the bottom, he peered around the corner.

He could see the door to the room with the glass box.

The cold barrel of a gun pressed against his neck.

'Don't move,' Connor snarled in his ear. He grabbed Jack's arm and, keeping the gun pointed at his head, marched him through the door into the main room and over to the glass hexagon.

Cloud opened the door and they went inside.

Hector had a satisfied smirk on his face as Connor removed Jack's backpack and tossed it into a corner.

Hector walked over to Jack and ripped the mask and AR Glasses off his head.

He stepped back and held up the mask. 'You really think I'm that stupid?'

Jack thought it best that he didn't respond to that question.

Hector grunted in disgust, dropped the mask to the floor and stamped on it.

Connor holstered his gun and forced Jack into a chair next to Slink, tying him to it with rope.

Slink nodded at Jack. 'All right, mate?'

Jack kept his eyes on Hector. 'Yep. You?'

'All gravy, baby.'

'Shut up.' Hector examined the AR Glasses.

As he slipped them on, Jack hoped that Obi had disengaged the map overlay.

Hector turned his head from side to side. 'These are very impressive.' He took the glasses off and examined the arms, where the microcomputer and transceiver were housed. 'Where did you get them?'

'A toy shop in Times Square,' Slink said, before Jack could come up with his own answer. 'We bought it on clearance for fifty quid.'

'Dollars,' Jack said.

'Yeah, right – dollars. Fifty dollars.'

Hector sighed, placed the glasses on the desk next to several chewing gum wrappers folded into origami animals and looked at Connor. 'You can go and round up the others now.' He glanced at one of the monitors in front of him. 'They're by the outer wall.' His gaze moved to Jack. 'Still stalling for time, are they?'

'What about the girl?' Connor said.

Hector frowned at the displays. 'She must be in the building somewhere. Go find her after you have the others. She can't do any damage – the generator is protected.' He clicked a mouse and brought up an image of the generator room.

Jack let out a small breath – Charlie had managed to keep out of sight of the camera.

But Hector had noticed Jack's reaction. 'I assume she's hiding somewhere,' he said in a flat tone. 'What was the plan, Jack?'

Jack shrugged and looked away.

Connor gestured for Monday to follow him, and the two men left the room.

Cloud stood behind Jack and Slink as Hector paced back and forth for a moment.

The stupid smirk on his face wouldn't go away. 'I've enjoyed the past few hours, Jack – our little game.'

Jack stared at him. 'Game? What game?'

Hector stopped pacing. 'Oh, come on, you are such a sore loser. Our game.' The smirk grew wider. 'The way that I pretended to leave a gap in the security like that.'

'Pretended?' Jack said, incredulous.

Hector rolled his eyes and turned the monitor so they could all see it properly. He brought up a complete map of the island, showing the camera positions and laser trip wires.

Hector clicked the mouse and a green line appeared. 'This is the path I left open through the security,' he said, as if talking to a child.

He pressed a button on the keyboard and the line vanished as several more cameras and trip wires engaged. Hector looked at Jack. 'The island is now on lockdown.'

A ring of red dots appeared, circling the island.

'And these are explosives, Jack. You try and escape, you'll trigger them and blow your legs off.' He turned the monitor back. 'Oh, and if you were wondering about the target I left for you...' He looked at Cloud. 'Show him.'

Cloud left the glass box and followed the power cables to the side door. She opened it wide enough for them to see inside. The cables ended and, as Jack had suspected, there was no generator.

But what did surprise him was that, apart from the narrow window high on the wall and a broken chair in the corner, the room was empty.

'Ta-da!' Hector grinned. 'There's nothing in there.'

'I didn't expect there to be,' Jack said, as Cloud returned.

Hector waved a finger at him. 'Yes, you did. You thought I'd set a trap, didn't you? Come on, Jack, admit it.'

Jack pressed his lips together.

Hector waved him off. 'You're so proud, aren't you? So...arrogant.'

Slink struggled against the ropes and tried to stand up, but Cloud grabbed his shoulders and pushed him back down.

'So,' Jack said to Hector, 'you've got us. What now?'

'Oh, I'm going to kill you,' Hector said, as if stating a simple fact.

Jack pretended to stifle a yawn. 'Is that all?'

Slink chuckled.

Hector's eyes flickered, but he kept his composure. 'I have something very special lined up for you.'

'Let me guess,' Jack said. 'You're going to make it look like some horrific accident.'

'No. I am going to get Connor to shoot you all in the head.'

This caught Jack off guard.

Hector's smirk returned. 'You and your little friends have been missing for years in London. So why would anyone notice you're gone now?' He glanced at Cloud, then back to Jack and Slink. 'Besides, no one here will even know who you are, even if they do eventually find your bodies.'

'Noble will know we're gone,' Slink said. 'He'll come find us. He'll work out what happened.'

'I will sort out that old man,' Hector said, looking at the computer on the back wall. 'Don't you worry – it'll all be taken care of.'

No doubt Hector was planning to set up Noble and get him put in prison for hacking or some other crime he didn't commit, Jack thought.

'What is it you're trying to do?' he said. 'Steal secrets like your dad started doing?'

Hector pulled his gaze from the computer. 'I'm not telling you my plans.'

'Why?' Jack said. 'Afraid we might put a stop to them?'

Hector shook his head. 'Far from it. I don't see the point in wasting any more time on you. You've been an irritant, but now it ends.'

CHAPTER FOURTEEN

JACK AND HECTOR STARED AT EACH OTHER AND the only sound came from the humming computer on the far wall.

Hector was so conceited – the way he thought everyone was under his control. *Just like his father.*

Something on the monitors caught Hector's attention. He smiled for a moment as he watched the screen, then looked up again. 'What do you think of this place?' he said, gesturing around him. 'The security is amazing. You have to admit that, at least.'

Jack shrugged. 'It isn't bad.'

'Isn't bad?' Hector's eyebrows rose. 'Come on, it's genius. Every angle covered.'

'Not every angle,' Jack said.

'Are you talking about the window you and your girlfriend climbed through?' Hector said. 'The way you set those dummies up and then danced between the cameras? You think I didn't leave that path deliberately for you to follow?' He balled his fists. 'You walked through the gap in the security that I'd left, Jack. Don't you get it? Once you were inside the building, I had Connor wait for you. *That* was the trap.' Hector drew in a deep breath and puffed out his chest. 'There was no other way in here.'

Jack held out his hands and gestured. 'And yet, here I am. Inside your top-secret room.'

Hector let out a short laugh. 'But I let you in here.'

Jack nodded. 'Yeah.' He glanced at the AR Glasses on the desk and the bag in the corner of the room. 'Everyone makes mistakes.'

Hector's face dropped. 'What?'

Jack drew in a breath, enjoying the moment. 'You say this is a game, Hector. Well, I hate to be the one to break it to you, but we're going to win it.' He glanced at Slink. 'Again.'

Slink grinned and winked.

Hector's eyes narrowed. 'No, you're not.'

'Hmm, yeah,' Slink said, 'we really are.'

Hector's jaw muscles flexed. 'I am going to enjoy watching *you* die first. You are very irritating.'

'I know,' Slink said. 'I work hard at it. But I'm afraid you're going to be in for a long wait.'

Hector glanced at Cloud.

Jack was sure he spotted the slightest flicker of self-doubt.

Jack lifted his chin and called out, 'Origami'.

The room plunged into darkness.

Hector roared.

Jack twisted his wrist and a blade shot out of his sleeve. He sliced back and forth a few times and cut through the rope, releasing his hands. He tapped Slink's leg, signalling him to stay put, then quickly cut the rope on Slink's wrist too.

Once free, Jack stood up. He listened for Hector as Cloud as they stumbled about, banging into things.

The room was pitch black, but he concentrated on the memory he'd spent the last few minutes building. In his mind, he could see his surroundings clearly and could picture the distance to each object.

Jack took two large steps forward, reached Hector's desk and went to grab the AR Glasses.

'Wait,' Hector snapped.

Jack felt a movement of air in front of his face and he jumped back. He took four quick steps to his left, getting out of the way of Hector and finding the nearest wall.

'Haven't you got a torch or something?' Hector shouted.

'No,' Cloud said. 'Wait, I can use my phone.'

Jack dropped to his knees as a faint light shone.

Slink leapt to his feet, snatched the phone from Cloud's hand and the room fell back into darkness.

'Get him,' Hector shouted.

There was a scuffling sound and a crash.

'Missed me!' Slink laughed. 'Whoops, and again.'

Jack stood and took five steps forward, until he found the corner of the room and his backpack.

He knelt down, unzipped the bag, pulled out a pair of night-glasses and slipped them on.

He stood, still holding the backpack, and turned around.

From his viewpoint, the room was now bathed in a green glow.

Hector and Cloud were shuffling around, their arms outstretched.

'Stay by the door,' Hector warned her. He found his desk, reached under it, pulled out a knife and started waving it about. 'Jack?'

As quietly as he could, Jack hurried to the custom computer and slid out a metal cylinder from his bag.

Following Charlie's earlier instructions, Jack wedged the cylinder between two of the computer's circuit boards, near a network hub.

Next he took the network cable out of his bag, plugged it into the black cube Charlie had also given him, then connected the other end to the computer.

He made sure the connection was secure and stepped back.

Obi would now be hacking into it, finding the evidence they needed to reverse all the damage Hector had done.

Jack spun around and looked at the AR Glasses on the desk.

Hector was still waving the knife around, blindly slashing the air. '*Jack*, I'm going to kill you.'

Keeping his back to the wall, Jack edged towards the desk but accidentally kicked a chair.

Hector wheeled round and lunged for him.

Jack spun to his left and ducked.

The knife missed him by a few centimetres and hit the glass wall above his head. Hector's arm buckled and he roared with a mixture of what sounded like pain and anger.

Jack sprang to his feet and ran forward. He made it to the desk and scooped up the AR Glasses. Then he grabbed hold of Slink and guided him to the door.

Cloud moved in front of them, her arms outstretched.

Jack pulled Slink behind him, letting Slink know that Cloud was there, then glanced around.

Hector was walking slowly towards them, swinging the knife back and forth, slashing the air and closing the gap.

Jack grabbed another chair, picked it up and slung it to his right. As it clattered off the glass wall, Cloud's head snapped in that direction and she went after it.

Jack pulled Slink to the door and they slipped through.

As they made their way across the room, carefully picking their way past debris, Jack glanced back – Hector and Cloud were still blundering about and had no idea Jack and Slink had made it out.

Jack stopped, pulled a key fob from his pocket and held it up.

He hoped Obi had managed to get the evidence they needed from Hector's computer.

Jack pressed the button and there was a huge snapping sound as sparks flew and thousands of volts of electricity tore through circuits.

Hector fell back, covering his eyes with his arm. 'No!' he screamed, but it was too late – Charlie's device had done its job – the computer was destroyed.

Hector roared and spun on the spot, looking like an enraged animal. 'I'm going to kill all of you.'

Smiling to himself, Jack guided Slink into the corridor.

But it wasn't over.

A gunshot rang out outside.

Jack and Slink hurried through a side door, out into the open air, and looked around.

Jack yanked the night-glasses off, slipped them into his bag and put on the AR Glasses in their place.

The green arrow appeared, showing him the path to follow.

'Charlie?'

'I'm almost at the rendezvous point,' she said. 'I was getting worried about you.'

'Never mind that,' Jack said. 'What about that gunshot?'

'I don't know. It must have been aimed at one of the others.'

Jack thought of Obi, Wren, Drake and Lux and knew that Connor wouldn't hesitate to kill any of them.

Slink looked at him. 'What do we do?'

'Stick to the plan,' Jack said. 'We'll go to the rendezvous point and meet up with Charlie and the rest.' Hopefully they'd all make it there in one piece, he thought.

Jack and Slink jogged right, following the green arrow between two crumbling outhouses.

With the cameras and security down, getting out would be a lot easier than it was to get in.

Jack and Slink hurried through the trees, making their way past a building that looked like a small church, and finally came to a clearing.

Jack was relieved to see several hooded figures waiting for them. But as he approached, his relief gave way to concern.

'Where's Obi?' he said. 'He's supposed to be back here by now.'

Drake shrugged and Lux shook her head.

Jack spoke into his microphone. 'Obi?'

There was no answer.

'We can't leave without him,' Wren said.

She turned to the path, but Jack spun on his heels – 'I'll go' and darted through the trees.

As he headed back around the main building, he spotted the beams of torches – one outside and one going into the building.

Jack squinted – Connor was going inside. That meant Monday was his only threat.

Good.

His size might slow him down if it came to a chase. Although Obi wasn't exactly Usain Bolt.

Jack jogged to the left, away from Monday, and headed to where Obi had patched into Hector's cameras.

Obi wasn't there. The cable he'd used to hack into the security swung below one of the cameras, but there was no laptop.

Jack turned slowly on the spot, his eyes searching. 'Obi?' he whispered.

Still no answer.

A torch beam swept past Jack, he dropped to his knees and watched as Monday walked through a clearing, scanning the trees and bushes.

Jack bit his lip. Where was Obi? Was he on the way back to the boat? Had he gone another way?

Monday kept going and soon vanished. At least if he was still searching, that meant they hadn't found Obi yet either.

Jack carried on around the main building.

There was a sudden roar. It sounded like Hector.

More lights appeared and several figures emerged from the building.

'Jack?' Hector screamed into the night.

Jack kept moving, away from Hector.

'Have you found Obi?' came Charlie's voice in his earpiece.

'No,' Jack breathed.

'What's he playing at?'

'Are you at the boat?' Jack whispered.

'Yeah. We're ready to go.'

Jack glanced back to see the figures had split up and were moving through the trees behind him. He picked up his pace, trying to put as much distance as he could between himself and Hector and his cronies.

At the building that looked like a church he stopped.

Was Obi in there? This was ridiculous.

Jack tried his headset again. 'Obi?'

'Jack?' Obi said in a whisper.

Jack let out a breath. Thank God, he was all right. 'Where are you?'

'In the glass room.'

'What?' Jack turned back towards the main building, keeping an eye out for Hector and his henchmen. 'Why? What are you doing?'

'No time to explain,' came Obi's faint reply. 'Just give me two minutes and get me out of here.'

As Jack approached the side door to the main building, there was no one around, so he ran inside, along the hallway and into the room with the glass hexagon.

There was a light on inside the structure.

As Jack approached, he saw Obi slip something into his bag and stand up.

Jack opened the door. 'What do you think you're –'

Obi put a finger to his lips and pointed to the doorway.

Several torch beams could be seen shining outside.

Jack spun back to Obi. 'Let's get out of here.'

The two of them raced across the room and back into the hallway.

'They're here somewhere,' they heard Hector snap. 'If you see them, you shoot, understand? I'll give you one hundred thousand for each body.'

'My pleasure,' Connor said.

Jack grabbed Obi's arm and pulled him up the stairs to the first floor.

They picked their way carefully along the corridor, heading for the window.

Obi let out a cry and Jack spun back in time to see Obi drop, his legs disappearing through the floor.

Jack lunged for him, but it was too late – Obi crashed through the ceiling below.

Jack crawled forward and peered down at him.

'Are you OK?' he whispered.

Obi groaned and sat up. 'I think so.' He struggled to his feet and dusted himself off. He was in a side room next to the main one.

Heavy footfalls sounded on the stairs, and the beams of torches bounced off the ceiling and walls.

'Go!' Jack shouted at Obi, pointing to a door.

Obi ran.

Jack stood and backed down the corridor as Connor, Monday and Hector came into sight.

Monday went to take a step forward, but Connor held him back and pointed at the hole in the floor. 'Careful.' He raised his gun at Jack. 'Come here.'

Jack continued to back away from them.

'I told you I wanted him dead,' Hector snapped. 'Just kill him.'

Jack turned and ran as fast as he could.

A shot rang out just as he launched himself through the window out into the open air.

Jack hit the ground, landing badly, and a sharp pain shot up his right leg. He crumpled, groaning.

Connor leant out of the window and fired again.

The bullet grazed Jack's arm.

He screamed out and scrambled back into the cover of the trees.

Another shot pierced the night, but this one thudded into a tree above Jack's head.

Jack dragged himself to his feet and the sharp pain tore up his leg again. He winced, clutched his arm and hobbled towards the beach.

It seemed to take for ever to reach the pontoon, but finally Jack spotted the boat and collapsed on the ground.

'Jack!'

Charlie and Slink ran over to him.

As they half dragged him to his feet, Jack said, 'Obi?'

'We've got him,' Charlie said, pointing at the boat.

Sure enough, Obi was sitting in one of the seats.

Shouts and torchlight came from behind them.

Charlie and Slink took an arm each and helped Jack into the boat.

Another gunshot rang out and a bullet thudded into the hull.

'Go,' Jack shouted.

Drake threw the boat into reverse, backed away from the island, then spun it around.

Several more shots hit the water around them.

'Hold on tight.' Drake rammed the throttle forward and the bow rose into the air.

As they sped away from the island, Jack glanced back.

Connor was waving his arms around, gesturing frantically at Monday.

Hector stood behind them, and his cold eyes followed Jack as the boat headed away in the sun's early rays.

After a few minutes, Jack allowed himself to relax. He hobbled to the stern of the boat and sat down with a heavy sigh. His leg hurt like mad. Mind you, so did his arm.

'Jack,' Charlie said, noticing the tear in his jacket and hoodie, 'did you get shot?'

'A little bit, yeah.'

'That's cool,' Slink said.

'It is not cool.' Charlie examined the wound.

'Chill,' Jack said. 'It's a scratch.'

Slink dropped to the bench next to him and looked from Jack to Charlie. 'So, I get how you fried Hector's computer with that thing you made, but how did you cut the power in the first place?'

'That was all Charlie's idea,' Jack said.

Using a knife, she had torn off a strip of Jack's shirt and was tying it around his arm. 'You know those cylinders Hector had next to the computer?' she said to Slink.

He nodded. 'Yeah.'

'Well,' Charlie said, 'Hector was feeding the computer with wireless power.'

'Wireless?' Slink said, looking dubious. 'Is that even possible?'

'Of course,' Charlie said. 'One day everything will be powered wirelessly.'

'That's amazing,' Wren said.

'Anyway,' Charlie continued, 'the generator was in the room behind the computer. Jack lowered me down into it, and then when he said the signal word – "origami" – I unrolled a sheet of wire mesh, blocking the power signal like a Faraday cage.'

Slink stared at her. 'Right...'

Jack glanced over at Obi. He was clutching his bag to his chest.

He looked at Jack. 'Sorry.'

'What were you doing?'

'You didn't give me enough time to copy the data Hector had gathered. I had to go in there and get his hard drive.'

'But you fried it,' Lux said to Charlie. 'Didn't you?'

'Yep,' Charlie said, looking at Obi. 'The data will be corrupted.'

Obi threw his bag down. 'Brilliant.'

'Next time,' Jack said, leaning back and wincing with the pain in his arm and leg, 'can you tell us what you're about to do?'

Obi hung his head. 'Sorry.'

'So,' Lux said. 'That's it? It's over?'

Jack nodded. 'Yeah, it's over.'

Slink let out a yell that made everyone jump.

'Come on, guys!' he said. 'We won. We finally beat Hector. No more stupid virus. No more supercomputers. It's over. We're done. We can go home.'

Everyone glanced at each other a moment, then simultaneously *whooped* into the faint dawn light.

• • •

Jack sat at the dining table in Serene's loft with the laptop from the Hollywood studio open in front of him. He stared at the blinking cursor in the password box.

'Are you going to hack into it?' Lux said.

He nodded.

'Then why are you hesitating?'

'I'm not sure I want to know what's on it.'

'Why not?'

Jack's eyes remained locked on the cursor. 'I've just got a feeling it might be –'

'Hey, all.'

Everyone looked up as Serene walked into the room.

'How was your trip?' Lux asked.

'Successful.' Serene dropped her bag on to the dining room table and looked at Jack. 'How's your mission going? Found your friend and sorted him out?'

'Yeah.' Jack smiled. 'We got him.'

Serene sighed. 'Thank heavens for that.'

Obi and Charlie came in from the gadget room.

'We got it,' Obi said.

Jack looked up at them. 'Got what?'

'We recovered the data off Hector's hard drive. It wasn't quite *that* fried. We can prove everyone he set up was innocent. Well, kinda innocent.'

'Great,' Jack said. 'Good work, guys.'

Serene looked between them all with a bemused expression. 'Care to explain what happened while I was gone?'

• • •

The next day, after plenty of sleep, Jack, Charlie, Obi, Slink, Wren, Drake, Lux and Serene went back to the warehouse outside New York.

Much to Jack's relief, the Shepherd had kept his word – the container was there with its ramp down, waiting for them.

Everyone said their goodbyes and Serene gave them all hugs.

'You remember to stay in touch.'

Wren smiled. 'We will.'

'When are you next coming over to England?' Slink asked.

'I'm not sure. Hopefully in the next month or two.' She looked at Jack and gestured to the laptop in his hands. 'Let me know how you get on with that Shepherd guy.'

Jack nodded and looked at Lux and Drake. 'If you ever come over, you're welcome to visit.'

Drake chuckled. 'Don't you live underground somewhere?'

'Yep.'

Lux smiled. 'I'll find you.'

Jack smiled back at her. 'I'm sure you will.'

Serene looked at the time on her phone. 'You have to go.'

Wren gave Serene, Lux and Drake another quick hug and the five Outlaws hurried up the ramp and into the container.

As Jack closed the door behind them, Obi said, 'Are we going to get knocked out again?'

'Hopefully *you* will,' Slink said. 'I'm not sure I can take eight hours of you telling us how great Lux is.'

Obi swung for him, but Slink jumped clear and laughed.

As they all strapped themselves into their upright beds, Jack thought of Hector. Was it really over? Would he give up on whole world domination?

Somehow, Jack doubted it.

CHAPTER FIFTEEN

BY THE TIME THE OUTLAWS GOT BACK TO London, Jack wanted nothing more than to go straight to bed and sleep for a few days, but they had a couple of things to do first.

The five of them were on a tube train as it travelled between stations.

Slink got to his feet.

'Where are you going?' Jack said.

'I'm getting off at the next stop, I need to go and see Mum.'

'We've got a little mission to do first,' Charlie said.

'I'll catch up later,' Slink said. 'I haven't spoken to her since we left Serene's.'

'She's fine.' Charlie gestured to the seat next to her. 'Please sit down. Noble has taken good care of her.'

Slink remained standing. 'How do you know that?'

'Come on, Slink,' Jack said. 'Just give us an hour, OK? It's important.'

The train stopped at the next station and the doors opened. Slink hesitated a moment, then sat back down next to Charlie. 'Fine. Sixty minutes, but that's all.'

• • •

Twenty minutes later, the Urban Outlaws entered a fully furnished apartment on the twentieth floor of a silver skyscraper in Greenwich.

Wren gasped and ran over to the huge windows in the main lounge. 'Look at this.'

The apartment had a view over the River Thames.

'What is this place?' Slink said, looking around. 'Does the Shepherd live here?'

Jack shook his head.

'Then who?'

'I do.'

They all turned to see a woman in an electric wheelchair sweep from the kitchen and into the lounge.

She had short curly hair, brown eyes and a wide smile.

Slink's jaw nearly hit the ground. 'Mum?'

'Hello, Tom.'

Slink hurried over to his mother and threw his arms around her. 'You're OK.'

'Of course I am.'

Slink pulled back. 'What are you doing here? Wait...What do you mean, you live here?'

Noble stepped from the kitchen with a cup of tea in his hands. 'Glad to see you all made it safely back home.'

Slink opened his mouth to say something, but Noble held up a finger.

'I was happy to help your mother move in.'

'Move...? Move in? W-what?'

Slink's mum looked at Charlie. 'Thank you so much for the chair, dear.'

Charlie smiled. 'That's OK.'

Slink looked at them in turn. 'Someone tell me what's going on!'

'Charlie adapted this wheelchair especially for me,' Slink's mum said.

'I went to Charlie's workshop in the bunker and brought it here,' Noble added. He looked at Obi. 'Good job you gave me the app to bypass the new cameras.'

'Watch this.' Slink's mum pressed a button and the chair lifted her almost into a standing position.

Part of the padded seat was now supporting her, along with a strap around her waist.

'Isn't this brilliant?' she said. 'Now I can reach things.'

'No need to modify the kitchen,' Noble said. 'It's fantastic.'

Charlie was blushing.

Slink didn't seem to know what to say. For the first time ever, he was speechless.

Slink's mum pressed a button and the chair lowered back to a normal seated position. 'This chair is a marvel.'

'I designed it to be a bit narrower than normal chairs too,' Charlie said. 'So it can go through doors.'

'Look.' Slink's mum pushed a lever sideways and spun the chair on the spot. 'You tell me how many others can do this?'

'Not many,' Jack said, grinning.

'Wait, wait, wait – we can't afford a place like this,' Slink said, gesturing around the apartment. 'Mum needs twenty-four hour care. The social services –'

'All paid for by a generous benefactor,' Noble said. 'You really don't need to worry, dear boy.'

Slink frowned. 'Who?' He turned to Jack, his face a wash of confusion.

Jack pointed at Obi.

Slink's eyes went wide and he spun to face him. '*You?*'

Obi shrugged. 'Jess said the business is doing really well. She's been putting money to one side for me. I haven't spent any of it and I didn't see the point in it piling up, so I –'

Slink leapt forward and threw his arms around Obi.

If Jack didn't know better, he could've sworn Slink was about to cry.

'Thanks, mate,' Slink whispered into Obi's ear.

Obi patted him awkwardly on the back. 'Yeah, like, y'know, no problem.'

Charlie leant in to Jack and whispered, 'We should take a picture. I've never seen that happen between those two before.'

• • •

An hour later, Jack and Charlie were outside the British Library.

Jack turned to her. 'Do you mind waiting here?'

'Huh? Why?'

Jack glanced at the brick building. 'I need to go in alone.'

Charlie's eyes narrowed as she considered him. 'Again? Why?'

'Just trust me, please?'

They stared at each other, and after a moment she exhaled. 'OK. But I'll be right here if you need me.'

'Thanks. I'll let you know what happens.' Jack marched into the library and found the same two thugs guarding the door to the reading room. He allowed himself to be patted down, then stepped inside and sat opposite the Shepherd at the table.

The Shepherd stared at him. 'Well?'

Jack slid the laptop towards him.

'I trust you haven't tampered with this?'

There was a short pause, then Jack said, 'Yep.'

One of the Shepherd's eyebrows rose. 'Excuse me?'

'Yeah, I had a look.' Jack crossed his arms. 'I had to. I told you I wanted to know who I was dealing with.'

The Shepherd stared at him a long moment, then said, 'I hope you're joking.'

'No joke,' Jack said. 'I've worked out who you are.'

The Shepherd remained frozen for a while, and then nodded. 'Go on.'

Jack took a breath. 'There were a few signs, but the laptop confirmed who you really are.'

'Did it? Well, what about the modified virus? Where is it?'

'You can't have it,' Jack said. 'We destroyed it.'

A grim smile swept across the Shepherd's face, then fell away. 'Very well.' He motioned to the door. 'You're free to go, Achilles.'

Jack went to leave.

'I hope we never cross paths again,' the Shepherd said.

Jack grabbed the handle and turned back. 'Oh, we will.' He nodded at the laptop. 'Because you owe me a favour.' He opened the door and left the room.

Back outside, he found Charlie.

'What happened?' she said.

'It's over.'

As they walked towards the main road, Charlie cocked an eyebrow at him. 'That easy?' she said.

'Have you got your phone on you?' Jack said.

'Yeah, why?'

'Do a search for that Alexandra Diamond we took off the guy on the train.'

'I already have, remember?'

'Just do it. Please?'

Charlie pulled out her phone. A minute later she gasped. 'Wait, that makes no sense.' She glanced at him. 'It says here that the Alexandra Diamond was returned to its original owner three days ago.'

Jack nodded.

'What's going on?'

'The Shepherd is part of the government,' Jack said.

'How can you know that?'

'He used us to get that diamond back because he didn't want to send his own people after it.'

'Why not?'

'I guess they don't want to get their hands dirty.'

'How did you know he was from the government?'

'The first clue was all that stuff we had to go through to get on to the plane.'

Charlie frowned. 'I wondered about that. Why make it so elaborate though?'

'Deniability,' Jack said. 'If we got caught, he'd deny all knowledge of us. Makes it look like we were just breaking in on our own.'

'What else?' Charlie said.

'I didn't tell you, but the Shepherd knew we were after Hector and the virus.'

Charlie scowled at him. 'Jack!'

'I know, I should've told you, but everything happened so fast. I'm sorry.'

'Go on,' Charlie said.

Jack continued. 'The laptop was the last piece of evidence I needed.'

They crossed the road.

'What was on it?' Charlie said.

'Names and bank account numbers.'

She looked at him. 'What for?'

Jack shrugged. 'My guess is they're the secret accounts of gun smugglers.'

Charlie nodded. 'That guy in Hollywood did have an accountant look about him.'

'I told the Shepherd I hacked into the laptop.'

'Why did you do that?'

'I wanted him to know that I'd copied the information.'

Charlie's eyebrows rose at this. 'But why? He'll see us as a threat.'

'No, he won't. He knows we're good guys; otherwise he'd never have contacted us in the first place.'

Jack glanced back at the library. 'By working out who he really is and keeping quiet about it, that means the Shepherd owes us a favour. A favour we might need one day.'

• • •

Back at the bunker, Jack was relieved to see that Obi had disengaged the extra security measures. He was sitting in his modified dentist's chair, talking quickly to Slink and Wren.

'What's going on?' Charlie said.

Obi glanced over at them. 'You'd better take a look at this.'

Jack stood behind Obi's chair and froze.

Cloud was on the main display. 'Hello.'

Jack's eyes widened. He glanced at Obi. 'Is this secure?'

'Of course. She can't trace us.'

'I don't want to trace you.' Cloud glanced around, seemingly nervous, then looked back at the camera again. 'I want to tell you something.'

Jack crossed his arms. 'If it's some stupid message from Hector, we're not interested.'

'No,' Cloud said, 'that's not it. I want you to know what Hector's planning next.'

'I don't care what he's planning,' Jack said. 'He's finished. It's over.'

'You will care when you hear about it.'

'Why should we trust you?' Slink said. 'This could be another one of Hector's traps.'

'I don't expect you to trust me that easily,' Cloud said. 'But I can prove I'm on your side.'

Jack's eyes narrowed. 'On our side? Really?'

'I knew you were following me. I deliberately dumped all those plans and receipts into that bin on the dock.'

'Yeah, right,' Slink said. 'You reckon you left a trail, do ya?'

Cloud kept her voice low. 'I did. And I have been helping you for some time. I also "dropped" that origami wrapper at the Del Sartos' apartment. I left the circuit board in the cupboard so I would have a reason to go back there. I could go on.'

Charlie snorted. 'Doesn't mean you've been on our side all this time.'

'I told you – I can prove it to you.' Cloud glanced around.

'You think we're that freakin stupid?' Slink said with a laugh. 'Come on, lady.'

Jack held up a hand and kept his gaze locked on Cloud. 'What's Hector doing?'

'Jack,' Charlie hissed, 'are you serious?'

'You can't trust her,' Wren said.

Jack ignored them and stared at Cloud. 'Well?'

Cloud leant in to the camera. 'When you hear what he's got planned, you'll have to act on it.'

'So what's his plan?'

Cloud took a deep breath and whispered, 'Have you heard of Medusa?'

Hang on for another wild ride with the next
heart-stopping book in the series:

URBAN OUTLAWS
COUNTERSTRIKE

The Urban Outlaws face their biggest
challenge yet. They must break in
to a mysterious, high-security facility
to secure the ultimate weapon:
Medusa.
But will Hector get there first?

www.urbanoutlawsbunker.com

THE URBAN

JACK

HACKER NAME: **ACHILLES**
REAL NAME: **JACK FENTON**
AGE: **15**
SPECIAL SKILL: **HACKING**
LIKES: **PHYSICS**
DISLIKES: **DUBSTEP**
GREATEST FEAR: **HEIGHTS**

CHARLIE

HACKER NAME: **PANDORA**
REAL NAME: **CHARLOTTE CAINE**
AGE: **15**
SPECIAL SKILL: **MAKING GADGETS**
LIKES: **COMPUTER GAMES**
DISLIKES: **GROSS HABITS**
GREATEST FEAR: **FIRE**

OUTLAWS

OBI

HACKER NAME: **OBI**
REAL NAME: **JOSEPH HARLINGTON**
AGE: **14**
SPECIAL SKILL: **SURVEILLANCE**
LIKES: **CONSPIRACY THEORIES**
DISLIKES: **SALAD!**
GREATEST FEAR:
ANYTHING THAT CRAWLS

URBAN OUTLAWS

SLINK

HACKER NAME: **SLINK**
REAL NAME: **TOM SMITH**
AGE: **12**
SPECIAL SKILL: **FREE RUNNING**
LIKES: **ART!**
DISLIKES: **QUIET DUBSTEP**
GREATEST FEAR: **NOTHING**

WREN

HACKER NAME: **WREN**
REAL NAME: **JENNIFER JENKINS**
AGE: **10**
SPECIAL SKILL: **DECOY/PICKPOCKET**
LIKES: **CARTOONS**
DISLIKES: **HOSPITALS**
GREATEST FEAR: **DROWNING**

URBAN OUTLAWS
CASE FILES
MISSION: KARMA

SERENE STOOD ON THE ROOF OF LONGWORTH House – an office building with stunning views over most of Washington DC, including the larger-than-life Capitol Building, with its dome lit up against the night sky.

But, it wasn't the sights that Serene had come for. She knelt down, checked the customised drill was in its cradle and then pressed the button. The motor whirred to life and the drill bit descended, sending a puff of concrete dust into the air.

When its task was done, Serene lifted the drill aside and unzipped a side pocket on her trousers. Carefully, she removed a roll of plastic explosives, slid it into the drill hole and inserted a remote detonator after it. Finally, she lifted a heavy, Carbon-Kevlar mat from her bag, and laid it over the hole.

Serene straightened up and took ten measured steps backwards. She held the detonator remote in her hand and hit the button.

A low *boom* rolled through the roof – the mat deadened the sound, but nothing could stop the vibration beneath her feet, or the large cloud of dust that billowed into the sky.

When the dust settled, Serene frowned for a moment, staring at the mat.

Had it worked? It didn't look any different.

She went to take a step forward, but leapt backwards as a huge chunk of the roof collapsed into the building.

The precision explosive had done its task, but wouldn't go unnoticed. She checked her watch – by her calculation, she had less than three minutes.

Serene turned around. Mounted to the wall behind her was a spool of rope. When she pressed a button on the back of her left glove, a length of rope slowly fed from the spool and she connected it to her harness. Serene then backed up to the edge of the hole and pressed the button again, feeding the rope out further and lowering her inside.

Once her feet had found solid ground again, Serene tapped the button on her glove again and the rope went slack, leaving her free to move about.

She was now standing in a large office. At one end was a table and six chairs; at the other, an antique desk with a painting hanging behind it. The painting was of geometric blocks of colour and, although it was impressive, and undoubtedly worth a fortune, it wasn't tonight's target.

Serene strode to the desk, heaved it aside and lifted a rug, revealing a slightly inset panel in the floor beneath. She slid the panel out of the way and shone her torch into the cavity. Below, staring back up at her, was the dial of a safe.

Serene opened a pocket on her arm, removed a black device with a small screen and a hole in the centre, and lowered it over the safe's dial. She then pressed a button and the screen sprang to life. The hole closed around the dial, and started spinning it back and forth.

Serene looked at her watch – two minutes.

The dial continued to spin and numbers scrolled down the device's screen.

Suddenly, the first one locked – eight.

Three more to go.

The device continued its task with quiet efficiency.

Serene was more than capable of cracking the safe the old-fashioned way, but why bother when a machine could do the task in half the time?

The next number, six, locked.

Serene stepped to the window and looked down. The street below was empty, apart from a white Lamborghini parked at the kerb.

The device beeped. She hurried back and lifted it out of the way. Taking a breath, Serene swung the safe open. She was pleased to see a single manila envelope inside. She took it out, quickly checked the contents, then slipped it under her jacket.

The door to the office flew open and two guards burst in, weapons drawn.

In one quick move, Serene unclipped a gun from her belt. But, instead of aiming at the guards, she spun on her heels, ran toward the window and pulled the trigger.

The glass shattered and she flung herself through and out into open air.

As she fell, Serene hit the button on her glove. She felt the rope tighten and slow her descent. By the time she reached the ground floor, she was falling at no more than five miles an hour.

Serene rotated her body and gently touched down.

She unclipped the rope from her harness and looked up at the guards. They both had a look somewhere between confusion and amazement.

Serene gave them a quick smile, then rushed over to the white Lamborghini and slipped behind the wheel. She hit the ignition, revved the car's engine to life, and raced away.

Thirty minutes later, the Lamborghini pulled into the forecourt of a fast-food restaurant and a guy in his early twenties climbed in.

Marley had dreadlocks, a beard, and his arms were covered in tattoos. He gave Serene a toothy grin. 'Problems?'

'No.' Serene handed him the manila envelope.

'Excellent.' Marley opened the folder on his lap and took pictures of each document with his phone.

When he was done, he handed back the envelope and winked. 'You were right – bad stuff in there.'

'How long?' Serene asked him.

'Already done. See for yourself.' Marley handed her his phone.

On the screen was the Cerberus forum and Marley had posted the pictures to a new thread. The title read, 'Congressman Kefer Accepted $2.8m in Bribes *Proof Here*' The documents showed a list of demands. The congressman had been accepting money from a gun manufacturer, in exchange for lucrative defence contracts.

'I sent a copy to the Feds too,' Marley said.

Serene smiled. 'Thank you.'

'Later.' Marley climbed out.

As Serene drove away, she smiled – *karma, delivered* – and wondered how the Outlaws were getting on with their mission.

PETER JAY BLACK loves gadgets, films and things that make him laugh so hard he thinks he might pass out. He went to Arts University Bournemouth and a career in IT followed. One day, a team of super-skilled kids popped into his head and, writing in a Hollywood apartment, he brought them to life. Peter lives in Dorset and in his spare time he enjoys collecting unusual artefacts like Neolithic arrowheads, ancient Egyptian rings and fossilised dinosaur poo.